SADDAM CITY

Mahmoud Saeed

SADDAM CITY

Translated from the Arabic by
Ahmad Sadri

SAQI

British Library Cataloguing-in-Publication Data
A catalogue record for this book is available from the
British Library

ISBN 0 86356 350 3
EAN 7-780863-563508

© Mahmoud Saeed, 2004
Translation © Ahmad Sadri, 2004

This edition published by Saqi Books, 2004

*The right of Mahmoud Saeed to be identified as the author of this work has
been asserted by him in accordance with the Copyright, Designs and Patents
Act of 1988*

Saqi Books
26 Westbourne Grove
London W2 5RH
www.saqibooks.com

Contents

On a Day like This

Monday… the first Monday of this ominous year.

I could never remember the date, let alone the day of the week, of important events in my life. This one, I would never forget.

It was early morning. My daughter Abeer asked:

– Dad, is today Monday?

Her brother Ammar laughed with derision:

– There is a smart question!

Abeer ignored him.

– On a day like this our Prophet was born. Dad, is it true that nothing bad happens to children on the day of the Prophet's birth?

I enjoyed hearing the tone of innocence in Ammar's attempts to assert his superiority:

– Oh, so that is supposed to be news? Everyone knows *that*!

I was hurrying them out the door. The sun shone pleasantly, deliciously. I found myself automatically putting on a light, summery outfit. Ammar's mother took exception:

– Are you forgetting that this is the dead of winter?

I smiled and let Ammar defend me:

– But Dad! You said that today would be warm. Besides, Kuwaiti TV is predicting warm, southwesterly winds for the entire day.

We all laughed.

– Don't forget the money. We better not leave it behind.

She took the envelope from the top of the chair, brought it to me and asked:

– Do you think he will finish building the house before the end of the month?

– The important thing is that we give him the money he's asking for. Let's leave the rest to him.

– I cannot believe we will be living in our own home. No more threats from 'the colonel', no more hassles with rented houses.

The money was around two thousand *dinars*.[1] I put the envelope beneath the driver's seat while waiting for the car to warm up. My wife was sitting next to me, but I could feel her heart beating beneath my seat where the money was. She kept urging me not to forget it, to remember to deliver it to the contractor. I kept nodding in fervent agreement after each drill. In the meantime the children, in the back seat, kept joyfully asking questions about the house and its size and beauty. I, however, was preoccupied with the few, not so financially comfortable, people from whom I had been forced to borrow, and about how I would return their monies and favors.

My wife got off in the old Basra quarter and I drove five minutes further to the al-Jazaaer circle to let the kids off near their school. Then I started in the direction of the courthouse. From there I had to go across the street to the coffeehouse, meet the contractor and go over the blueprints of the house – blueprints for the dreams of the entire family. But he was not there. I decided to hand over the money to his assistant. I did this

---

1. At the time of this novel, 1979, an Iraqi *dinar* was equal to US $3.20.

without counting it, as I was in a great hurry to get back to school to ratify my one-hour leave, which I had obtained the previous day. I told the assistant I would be back in fifteen minutes.

How stunning was this sun, this warmth that filled the world. The only thing marring the day was the rainwater from a couple of days earlier. It had covered the streets with a cake of mud that was now being pulverized by speeding cars to create clouds of dust.

In front of the Census Bureau the car started to sputter. It coughed a couple of times and died. I tried to fire it up repeatedly but failed. Kaput. A dead heap of junk. I got out to push it off the road. A bunch of giggling students joined in to help while making fun of the car in whispering tones followed by chuckles. I thanked them. We were all panting.

The breeze was sweet and cool; I wiped the sweat from my forehead. Monday! The day of the Prophet's birth! Was it a good omen? Earlier, Abeer and Ammar were quarrelling over the proper honorific for the Prophet. Was it 'May God Bless and Greet Him' or just 'Peace Be Upon Him'? I did not make a habit of sounding such depths.

I locked the car and took the bus. Standing among the crowd of passengers I suddenly remembered I did not have exact change for the ride. But a man with a long face and prominent nose paid my fare. Who was he? His face did not ring a bell. But there it was: a simple problem solved. A good omen? Yet the image of the dead car tugged at my heart. I would have to start looking for an honest mechanic. And what a labor that would be!

In the mirror, my eyes met those of a young female student. From the faculty of education, no doubt. A slight shiver went up my spine. Twenty years ago such an encounter would intoxicate me beyond measure. It would stroke my ego and evoke dreams of grandeur. But what remained today? A thinning forehead, whose severity was somewhat softened by a pair of still, soulful eyes. I got off the bus.

The traffic cop in his box, with his white helmet, slightly bulging belly and falcon eyes personified the system he served as he labored to inspire fear in hordes of unruly drivers. Then I chuckled at his name tag: *Mr. Pitiful*![1] My smile lingered. I felt crowded by everything around me. My lungs were awash in the tempting aroma of tea coming from the new coffeehouse in front of the Hamdaan Hotel. Then my heart sank. I had left all that money with a man I did not know or trust! Nor had I insisted on a receipt! The only proof of the transaction was his conscience. What if he denied the whole business? I was suddenly drenched in perspiration. This was the last instalment, made up of borrowed money. If I lost it, all our dreams would be lost. The only thing to do was hurry and get to the contractor and his assistant before the devil got there.

I reached the gates of the school. Something, which in my haste I failed to grasp, forced me to take a detour, a near-complete circle around the gates, before entering. I took the permission for my one-hour leave out of my pocket. Abd al-Raheem, the janitor, was smoking. He smiled and returned my greeting.

– The dean is asking for you.

– Who? Has Dean Idris returned from his vacation?

He looked nonplussed, as though he had been caught committing a sin.

– No. The vice-dean, Muslim Ali, is looking for you.

I laughed.

– And what does he want to squeeze out of the morning?

– God only knows.

I had entered the room when the dark, foreboding tone of the preceding conversation hit me. The vice-dean did not return my

---

1. '*Miskeen*'.

greeting. Instead he softly gestured toward a couple of strangers in the room with the air of performing a sacred duty for the good of all. I felt a strange charge of urgency in the air.

– These gentlemen are looking for you.

One of them was a fat, olive-skinned man with a huge belly. Next to him sat a short, compact, dark fellow whose dead, light-brown eyes were brimming with some inner torment. I smiled again.

– Fellowship and peace to you!

Muslim Ali introduced me:

– This is Mustafa Ali Noman.

The men stood up at once. Their faces were ashen. Could I inspire such fear? I was a simple, peaceful man, loved by children and incapable of scaring a kitten. Were they preparing for a confrontation? But with whom? The fat man said:

– Shall we?

His right hand was showing the way out. My head was racing with scenarios. Maybe they intended to inquire about one of the students; maybe there was some property affair to be settled. I walked ahead of him. He stopped by the main gate. Abd al-Raheem was still blowing clouds of smoke from his cigarette. A couple of my friends, Mohsen Abellah and Mohammad Saaei, cheerfully greeted me as they whizzed by, skipping the stairs three at a time.

I turned eagerly to my fat interlocutor.

– I am at your service.

– Please come with us, sir.

– But where?

– A simple interrogation … Just a few minutes.

– *Interrogation?*

It was as though I had been slapped by the word. I tried to catch my breath.

– But who are you?

– Security.

I went with them toward the gate as frantic questions gnawed at me. Why not go with them? I was innocent. I knew myself better than anyone in this world.

– Are you positive I am the one you are looking for?

– Mustafa Ali Noman?

– Yes.

The fat agent bent his head slightly, indicating I was the one, and added:

– A few minutes only.

He spoke these words in a practiced monotone, as though he had repeated them many times before finally memorizing them.

– Why don't you interrogate me here?

He forced a pale, sallow smile while pointing to the car that had been parked inches from the school's front gate, apparently to block a fleeing suspect. This was why I had been forced to go around the gate earlier.

– We have our orders.

The smaller fellow sat behind the wheel. I climbed into the front seat followed by the other agent. I was being squeezed toward the windshield of the small pickup truck from the few inches of the front seat that the fat behinds of my flanking guards had left me. I must have meant a great deal to them, because the fat agent heaved a loud sigh of relief as he shut the door on his side of the car. He then extended his hand to hold my shoulder as if I was a small sparrow capable of flying out the small window. The driver assumed a gloomy and pallid face as though he were a thief who had stolen a sacred object. Then I noticed that the hard-breathing fat agent was wearing a fake smile to cover up what was obviously a great deal of fear. The thought occurred to me that we were all suffering in the clutches of the same dark destiny. This realization gave me confidence. I laughed and said:

– You are surely mixed up about my identity …

They did not acknowledge my words. They had captured their prize and did not see the point of speaking much. Then the fat agent turned to me with the air of being in possession some kind of privileged intelligence:

– Where is your … umm, red VW?

The pettiness of the question sickened me. I shot back:

– Dead.

The Gates of Hell in Basra

We reached the unfinished structure of the National Television Station. I also saw my children's school from there. Later, when I tried to recall my last impressions of freedom, I was rankled by the cold, empty shapes of these two buildings. Then we turned into the street at the back of the Security Headquarters.

– Get out of the car.

The fat agent had barked the order at me, and then quickly disembarked. We were inside a huge garage. Behind us the gate had already been shut and a pale, armed man was guarding it. The sound of the gate locking separated us from the world of the ordinary. We had entered a terrifying secret underworld.

As soon as I got out of the car, it drove off to find its place among the endless rows of parked cars. It was hard to imagine so many cars in one place in the middle of the cramped quarters of the downtown Basra. Was this the same ordinary building whose façade was indistinguishable from the others? Who owned all these expensive cars, glittering under the metal roof of this massive lot?

– Come along.

Another man standing by the car issued the next order. I turned to him. He was standing in a huge, unpaved yard with a door leading to a flight of stairs. In it stood a man wearing a thick, dark-colored blindfold and his hands were tied behind his back. It looked like an agent was questioning him. This filled me with terror. My eyes were glued to the man under interrogation. The order was repeated:

– Come along.

My attention returned to myself. I was breathing hard. A man in his thirties with ordinary features and civilian clothes stood in front of me. He wore a dark pea-green jacket and there was plenty of joy in his eyes. My state of shock and fright seemed to please him.

– Step forward.

I opened my mouth to ask him a question, but a different one emerged:

– What are you going to do?

– Blindfold you!

His tone was enough to convince me that a dark, ineluctable fate had swallowed me whole. He had bent down to the ground to fetch a piece of grimy cloth from lying partly in a pool of stale water produced by a dripping faucet in the wall. He picked up the cloth that was dripping with filth and shook it. Muddy droplets flew in all directions. I wailed from the bottom of my heart:

– Please, let that be! Tear the sleeve off my shirt and use it as a blindfold.

– How about your tie then?

Why had I not thought of that?

– No problem.

I untied the tie and let it turn into an executioner's instrument. He tied it hard around my head, crossing it several times over my eyes. Thus I was hurled into a world of perils through the main gate.

– Turn around.

I had no choice. A ghastly pair of cold bracelets jingled around my wrists and clicked shut. Where did they come from? I had not seen them in his hands when he was blindfolding me. They must have been of the best quality. I immediately felt the blood choke around my wrists. I remained in my place for a short spell. The blindfold pressed on my eyes. Then a coarse hand grabbed my arm and gently guided me forward:

– Here is a flight of stairs ... Climb ...

The tie was made of thick silk, and although it was coiled three times around my head and over my eyes, it failed to cover the space between my nostrils and the corners of my eyes. There remained a couple of small merging triangles from which I could see my feet. I climbed three steps and turned to the right, then climbed three more steps. We must have arrived at an enclosed space as the humidity and heat increased. My guide left and I stopped, feeling a pang of pain in my shoulder due to the tight grip of the handcuffs. How long did I stay there? Time slows down in the presence of pain. I was reminded of the theory of relativity.

– Aiiieeeeee!!!!

A hideous scream echoed from the bowels of the building. It had to have come from somewhere nearby. Another long howl followed, then a third one. I could hear heavy breathing; a worn-out, irate voice snarled:

– This one passed out. Get a doctor.

A knock on my shoulder clued me that I was being addressed.

– What is your name?

– Mustafa Ali Noman.

This was followed by the heaviest, most unexpected slap, which opened up my right eye. I felt a warm paste gluing the tie to my eye.

– Why are you so stuck up? Who the hell do you think you are? Herr Professor from the University?

– Who ... ? Me ... ?

How could someone in my position be stuck up? I was fighting wild vertigo when a second, more powerful blow landed in the same place on my face. I was thrown back. For some reason I had thought I had been standing atop a flight of stairs and feared I would fall, but I hit a wall instead. I rested my head and upper back on the wall. The sticky paste was blocking my tiny field of vision. Why this violence? What had I done? Another loud, sharp voice with an effeminate ring asked:

– What is your complete name?

– Mustafa Ali Noman ...

– Confess!

– To what?

– You don't know to what?

I enunciated with the kind of patience and clarity I did not know I could muster.

– Help me.

Yet another voice intoned:

– Fine. Take him away!

I felt a heavy hand taking my forearm and pushing me a few steps. My right eye was still bleeding. The tie could no longer absorb the blood flow. From the corner of my other eye I saw blood dripping on my shoes. The pain in my shoulders was unbearable; it felt like two patches of fire.

– Stop... Here... Turn around... To the right.

A push to the front. A sudden halt. Then another push, followed by a second halt.

– Mustafa Ali Othman?

I shook my head.

– No. My name is Mustafa Ali *Noman*.

– Makes no difference.

– May I request that you loosen my handcuffs a bit?

– How many times have you been abroad?

– Once only, and that was on government business.

– Tell the truth.

– I swear by the glorious God.

– How many years did you spend in Sulaymaniyah?[1]

– In Sulaymaniyah?

– Yes.

– I did not spend years there!

– Have you never been there?

– Yes, I have.

– How long did you spend, then?

– A couple of hours.

– Are you joking?

– It's the truth.

– What did you do there?

– We ate at a tourist restaurant and then left.

– Are you telling the truth?

– Yes.

– But you deny using an assumed name.

– An assumed name?

– Your name is Mustafa Ali Othman, but you call yourself 'Noman'.

– But that's an error! As I've said, my name *is* Mustafa Ali Noman.

– How do you know Rafaat Jaboori?

– Never heard of him.

The questioning reverted to my trip abroad. I smiled as I became convinced they had mixed up my name with someone else's. I gathered all my courage and eloquence to assure them that they had made a mistake, and added a request that they turn my car keys over to my family.

– Take him out of here.

_____

1. An area in the northern, Kurdish part of Iraq.

18

I pleaded and implored, but was not heard. I was led away the same way I had come and entered a long passage that appeared to connect several rooms. Then I descended a few steps, felt cold air on my face and guessed that I was in the same yard where I had been blindfolded. I was taken down another few steps, where it was extremely cold and damp. A door was closed behind me and a key turned in the keyhole. Another, less violent, hand took hold of my arm and guided me along.

– Sit on the ground.

From the small triangle of vision I saw a filthy cement floor. I asked:

– May I stay standing?

– Why?

– I suffer from chronic dysentery, and sitting on a cold surface can bring on an attack.

– OK. Sit down for now until I come back with permission for you to stay standing.

I squatted to prevent my skin from touching the cold floor. A gentle pressure on my shoulders pushed me down.

– Sit cross-legged. Are you afraid to soil your fancy suit?

He chortled at his own wit. I gathered that that was the only permitted sitting position in this prison. Meanwhile, the pain from the handcuffs was positively burning the flesh around my shoulders. I was sure that sitting on the cold floor would bring on the worst attack of dysentery. It had been a long time since I had crossed my legs. Besides, I found it hard to cross my legs from a squatting position without the use of my hands. They probably amused themselves watching people in a fix like this. I tried to sit on the floor while thinking about what I would do if I got the runs behind locked doors. I would rather have died first. Then I heard a voice:

– OK. Let him stand.

– Stand up.

Who was this one? I thanked God and shuffled to my feet, stumbling and reeling as I was unable to use my hands for balance. The blindfold had slipped a little from my eyes, and I could see by tilting my head. I was afraid I would be noticed and insulted again. So I asked the guard to fix my blindfold, which he did. Then I leaned on the wall. My thoughts reverted to the money I had left with the contractor's assistant. I did not trust builders. Weren't Freemasons all builders too? If he should deny receiving the money, the whole world would crumble on my head. I would lose everything.

The time was past ten in the morning already. I assumed they were re-investigating my identity as they left me there. This would take a few hours, if not more. They had found me under my real surname, so perhaps they would check with the school again to confirm that my name had always been Ali Noman and not Ali Othman. It was no doubt a typo. In the past I had made the same sort of mistake myself and even taken pains to point out my own error; I made a habit of empathizing with the shortcomings of others by recalling my own.

I began secretly exercising to help circulate the blood in my shins. When the pain became intolerable in one foot I would stealthily shift my weight to allow a temporary sense of relief. This reminded me of running to school when I was little. By the time I got to school I would feel that my shins were exploding. The pain in my shoulders started to spread to my spine. I wondered how long I had stayed in that position and how long I could stand it. I'd heard a man could withstand more hardship than he expects. I had to take myself to the limit. Sitting down would have brought relief, but who would open the doors for me if I got the runs? I would soil my clothes and bring a flood of insults down upon my head, which I would not be able to endure.

The din of groans, cries, shrieks and supplications battered my ears. The direction of these noises led me to suspect that my dungeon was connected to others on upper levels. I was probably being watched from openings in the ceiling. Every so often a deep, agonizing scream would tug at the strings of my heart. At times like this the other cries sounded like a ghastly background chorus from another world.

I was shaking uncontrollably. The sound of approaching footsteps caused me to prepare for another blow. I guessed it was past noon and once more, I thought of my children at school, soon to expect me back home. What would my poor wife do? How long would she wait before taking a taxi to pick up the children? How would she deal with her worries? In whom would she find solace? She would probably go to my brother-in-law Hussein and his wife Zeinab – as though the troubles of 'nationality'[1] status were not enough for them!

The heavy metal door opened, and more than one set of footsteps drew near.

– This way. Come along. Sit down.

They brought another person; I expected them to seat him near me. The aperture of vision under the blindfold was becoming clearer despite the swelling in my cheek and eye. I thought I could see the new inmate if I raised my head just slightly, and tried it.

– Lower your head, you dirty dog! You son of a bitch!

I regretted having instigated this new volley of insults and decided not to use my crooked angle of sight any more.

Slowly I came to the conclusion that the matter did not involve any confusion about my name. If so, they would have

---

1. The Baath Party deported several waves of Iraqi citizens to Iran on charges of Iranian ancestry. The relatives of those deported were themselves branded as being of dubious 'nationality', and blacklisted for future deportations.

cleared it up after a couple of hours. The problem of 'nationality' could not be the cause of my arrest either, or they would have brought up Hussein's name. I sneaked a look at the watch of the new inmate who sat to my right. It was past 1 PM. This was what I had guessed. They opened the metal door and then another door.

– Hurry up!

They began calling names:

– Mofid Yaseen! Miri Abbas! Nateq Malek …!

I tracked the names into the fifties before losing count. The first cell was locked. A second was opened and the recitation of names continued. Then the second cell was closed and a third that was near me was opened. Thus, it appeared that this vestibule in which I was kept opened onto three huge collective cells. What could be the crimes of so many prisoners?

My pains increased. The numbness started to paralyze my entire arm. The burning sensation was scorching my bones. For a few seconds I really wished I could die and escape the shooting pains. As daylight started to fade, the yellow light of the lone light bulb in the vestibule became more prominent. The number of people in the vestibule had increased. I guessed there were seven people there. It was some time after five o'clock when the third cell was locked. I gave in to the darkest despair. Why had they asked me about Sulaymaniyah? Who was Rafaat Jaboori? These questions indicated some identity mixup. But demanding confession meant there was an accusation. Had they not beaten me? I felt the prick of a sharp pain at the top of my spine.

Despite my apprehension I raised my head to look at the new inmate. I could not believe what I saw. A man sat cross-legged, leaning against the wall, his head and face heavily bandaged. Nothing was visible of his face except a couple of huge nostrils. The bandage was stained with blood that spread in all directions. The bandage around his mouth and beard was wet with saliva. This was why they blindfolded the prisoners: so as not to see things like that.

What had I done? With whom had I associated to cause this misunderstanding? Was Jawaad Kazem the reason for all this? He was not my friend, just a good neighbor. I did not know him well, nor did we meet on a regular basis. He was a diminutive, well-mannered man with three sons. There was a rumor that he was a leftist. He had refused to join the Baath Party. In retaliation he was transferred to Faw Island.[1] According to his wife the pressure to join the party resumed at Faw, and his life had been threatened. He had subsequently given up and joined. Jawaad Kazem used to visit with his family during holidays. I once ran into him near the Karnak movie theatre. He was carrying a bag full of fresh Zubeidi fish. I gave him a ride, and later they sent us a plate of cooked fish. Around a month later his weeping wife showed up at our door around midnight. It is not easy to describe the defeat that filled her eyes. Her husband had not returned home. His colleagues on Faw had seen him get on the bus to Basra, and another friend saw him at the Omm al-Broom bus terminal there. He had disappeared between Omm al-Broom and his house. Kazem's wife asked me for help, and I put myself at her disposal. She suggested we check police stations and hospitals. Throughout our rounds that night she kept crying for her children, whom she'd left alone at home. Our search came to naught. We might as well have gone whaling in the Tigris. I gave up on the police stations when we finally met an empathetic sergeant who gently shook his white head and averted his eyes.

– Don't bother searching for him with us.

He then left the room abruptly, without telling us how to search for him. Apparently even this cryptic response was quite indiscreet. We were dismayed by the cold, routine treatment we

---

1. A small, remote island by the mouth of the Persian Gulf.

received at the hospitals, where we were dismissed with barely a note of sympathy. We were no more than the latest link in a long chain of people who visited hospitals vainly inquiring about missing loved ones.

At 3:30 AM we returned home empty-handed. I did not sleep for a few hours, but then passed out. We resumed the search the next day. The kids appeared to know more than I expected. Twenty-five days later an officer brought Kazem's wife a permission slip to look for her husband's body at the morgue. This time their next-door neighbor Muhammad Ali accompanied her. He told me there were more than thirty people waiting in line. Kazem's body had been dismembered in four pieces, but the blood was thoroughly washed off. I begged him to stop describing the scene; I could not believe that the serene, smiling man I had known could die such a horrible death.

Could that night of searching for Jawaad Kazem have counted against me? But they did not ask me about him. They asked me about this Jaboori character instead, whom I did not know. What was my charge? I never interfered in politics. True, I hated the Baath, and my wife was a 'nationality'. When I met my friends by chance, we would drink and talk about life in general, and only occasionally about politics. Of course we, like most everybody in Iraq, were bound by a common (but often silent) hatred of the Party. This reminded me of the meetings a group of us held once or twice a month. My group of friends included Abu-Wael and Hussein. But this tradition ended due to the scarcity of alcohol. Indeed, lively meetings of any kind became a thing of the past as we all feared that casual conversations would lead to politics. The risk was too great.

At our last meeting Hussein related that in the al-Zubeir neighborhood of Basra, a student from a Mosuli[1] family had come to visit with his uncle. The student was later arrested as he

---

1. A city in Northern Iraq.

and his friends were praying. His uncle, a civil engineer working for the city, went asking after his whereabouts with some indignation. He was told that 'the kid belongs to a religious organization'. The uncle had retorted:

– What of it? It beats belonging to an infidel organization!

Three days later the uncle's body was turned over to his family.

Events like this happened routinely, but we kept our peace. For the simple folk, silence is more eloquent than words. Life became crueler as the days passed, and the risk of uttering a single word in the midst of so many amateur spies increased daily. Had anyone reported Hussein's story? If so, I would have been asked about it; no, it could not be.

The time was past six o'clock in the evening. The cruel insistence on extracting every last bit of information from the inmates had increased. With the rising tide of supplications, shrieks and howls of pain I thought I was going to lose my mind. My feet were freezing, but my shins, shoulders and spine were aflame with pain. There was nothing to do but wander in a field of memories in search of what might have triggered my arrest.

We used to spend time every Thursday at our club, the Teachers' Union. Once Hussein asked:

– Why on earth do we come here every week?

– Where else do we have to go? It is our union, after all.

– But it is filthy and it crawls with informers.

– And we have a choice, no?

This was a tongue-in-cheek rhetorical debate between Hussein and Abu Wael.

– Aren't we members of the Teachers' Union?

– We are!

– So why didn't the union stand up for you when you were fired? Why did the president of the guild refuse even to meet with you, as you requested?

– You know that he is a loser and a drunk.

– The union elections were conducted right here, and there were more security agents than voters.

Hussein pointed to where the agents had been placed.

– Here was one, here sat the other one, and there stood another one. The ballot box was placed here, near the TV set. When we wrote down the name of a candidate on the ballot, one of the security agents would check it, although there was no candidate competing against the slate of 'the gangsters'.[1] And if you refused to vote you would be sent to jail. Look at this union! It's supposed to be one of the largest and richest guilds. It might as well be the lair of highway robbers; it's infested with foreign snitches. If the elections were free, the only ones who would have voted for its current president would be the minister of education and his political deputy.

We laughed heartily. During this exchange I kept an eye on those around us, especially on those who appeared to be nationals of other Arab countries; the regime usually hired agents from amongst them. But no one was eavesdropping. Most were mired in their own grinding troubles. There was no way this conversation was reported. And if it had been, they would have asked me about it, too.

After an hour the din of torture started to die down, except for an occasional primal scream. Then a different kind of voice came to hold sway over the dungeons. First a gentle voice started reciting the opening chapter and the Victory Chapter from the Qur'an. The same voice was then heard praying. Then he resumed his soft, enthralling recitation:

– *When there comes succor of Allah and victory. And thou dost see men entering the God's religion in droves. Then recite*

---

1. That is, the Baath Party.

thanks to thy Lord and pray for His forgiveness, for He is most merciful.[1]

This gracious, warm voice reverberated through the cells. Then another voice was heard reciting a different part of the Qur'an; then a third and fourth joined in. Soon tens of voices were reciting, none marring the clarity and beauty of another. Here was the eloquent, peaceful, defiant voice of the subjugated and disenfranchised.

I had never been a practising Muslim. But the recital of the Victory Chapter brought back fond memories of my father's calm, enchanting nightly prayers, and this somehow soothed the sharp pain in my shoulders and shins. Why did I feel so close to these people? Maybe it was because we were all victims of the same supreme injustice.

Here the recitations stopped. It was past nine o'clock.

– Abdel Amir! … Abdel Amir!

This was the voice of the henchman. After the exquisite recitations it struck me as the barking of a rabid dog.

– Open this door.

A man was being kicked down. I felt exposed.

– Sit down.

There was another thump. Someone else was thrown on the ground. I heard heavy breathing. The two guards on duty were engaged in a conversation.

– Today is Monday.

There was a pause.

'On a day like this, our Prophet was born …' Oh, voice of torment! 'Is it true that nothing bad happens to children on a day like this?' Ammar was laughing. Taking his cue from me, he responded, 'Old wives' tales, one and all. Dad knows. Who has filled your head with all this superstition? Dad! You tell her.'

---

1. From Chapter 110 (*al-Nasr*) of the Qur'an.

– Tomorrow I will be out with her in the al-Maghaayez market.

The voices of the guards brought me back to the prison. One of them started to make fun of those who had recited the Qur'an. He began to put on an obscene performance in the style of Shi'ite *mullahs* reciting the passion of Imam Hussein in the Battle of Karbala:

– The Imam entered the quarters of his sister Zeinab and took off his clothes and addressed her ...

But he failed in his attempt to provoke the prisoners by insulting their religious beliefs. Like a dog that does not know when to stop barking, he kept up his vain act until he went hoarse and shut up.

Another entreating voice came from the cells in the upper floor:

– I am the cousin of Najm Sharif![1]

– Damn your father *and* Najm Sharif's father!

With nightfall the voices finally started to die down. But I did not lower my guard. Then I heard the sound of footsteps, followed by a sharp sigh.

– What is your job?

– I am a builder.

– Twenty *dinars* a day. So why do you want more?

Another series of footsteps approached.

– And you?

– I?

– Yes, you.

– I am a teacher.

– All the trouble starts with the teachers. Are you not a member of the Baath Party?

– Yes ...

– Aaiiiiieee! ... For God's sake ...!

---

1. An official in the Baath Party.

This last scream came from the grates in the ceiling. Someone could be heard walking away. I felt relieved. The silence started to thicken, and my pain deepened. I remembered my allergic foot. Would I have an attack? If so, how would I be able to scratch it with my hands tied behind my back? A fuse of pain was burning its way through my shoulder and down into my arms.

One of the guards was singing:

– *Oh brown sweetie, tell me, tell me …*

Is it possible that a henchman would enjoy a ballad like that?

– *You are my torment …*

The words were banal but his voice was warm. He kept switching from song to song, keeping the beat with his foot in the style of the al-Khashabah folk performers. His tone betrayed a note of primitive originality, a sort of curious, deep-rooted, homey spirit. How had someone like him ended up in an inferno like this?

What are Ammar and Abeer doing now? How did they spend this wretched day? And if I followed the path of Jawaad Kazem, to whom would my wife turn? Hussein and Zeinab, undoubtedly, at this hour of the night. They would probably start where I had started with Kazem's wife: police stations, hospitals, and administrative detention centers. They would return empty-handed, as we had done.

Abu Wael was an old revolutionary. I recalled what he had told me during one drinking bout:

– I was imprisoned during the time of the king and also during the reign of Abdulkarim Qasim, and later during the ill-omened Ramadan.[1] But what I underwent during the third arrest was worst than anything I had seen before. For the first time in the history of Iraq the hands of those arrested were tied behind

---

1. The 1963 Baath Party *coup d'état*.

their backs. We had seen this in newspaper reports from Vietnam. The very act of tying one's hands in this way for a long time constitutes a form of torture. But hanging a handcuffed victim from the ceiling would lead to only one of two results: giving in and confessing to whatever is required, or death. There is no other choice.

– And did you confess?

– Oh, I confessed, all right. But more than you can imagine died under torture.

My fear increased. Would they hang me from the ceiling?

– The idle gossip gets in our way. Otherwise, I would come crawling to you, little darling.

I could no longer resist the pain. I had had enough. When would I scream with pain? Why had I worn this light outfit? I felt the cold in my bones and tried to relax my feet. Another hour passed. It was midnight. What a miracle! I had suffered and endured for fourteen hours. My body was getting numb, but I would sooner pass out than sit on the ground willingly. I would not bring on an attack of dysentery: on a cold night like this I would not regress to the helpless creature that I had been thirty-five years ago during an attack.

– The gang leader[1] was personally in charge of our torture. We were in Karak then. The first thing he did was pull out a member of the central committee and shoot him in front of us. Imagine. We compromised and struck a deal with him, shook hands with him. So many of us were killed by those filthy hands.

If only I had kept the money at home! Then the house could have been finished, and I would have had something to leave my poor kids and their widowed mother. The kids must have been asleep by then, but I knew their mother. She would not sleep. Even if she went to bed, those beautiful eyes would stay open, crying until the tears dried. What would she say if the kids

---

1. That is, Saddam Hussein.

insisted on an answer? Anything but the truth. And how would she know the truth? Who would tell her the truth other than Kazem's wife?

Minutes passed like years. At two in the morning the sound of turning keys and iron doors rolling on their hinges preceded the sound of heavy, nailed boots.

– A routine roll call.

The voice was devoid of emotions.

There were thirty-five in the first collective cell, forty-two in the second, sixty-six in the third. There were eight in the vestibule where we were.

– All set.

The heavy steps approached. I trembled. They did not intend to do anything with me yet. There was a sound of handcuffs opening.

– Get up, you. On your feet. Spread this. You, come here.

I awoke from my shallow stupor and tried to feel with all the senses left to me. The handcuffs locked again.

– You, come here.

This time I was being called. I took a few steps toward the source of the voice, staggering; my feet could not carry me.

– Turn around.

The handcuffs were opened, and someone pulled my right hand forcefully. I screamed. It was as though he were pulling my arm from its bony socket. Were they going to hang me from the ceiling? Could I possibly endure that? I had spent the last ten hours dreaming of someone unlocking my handcuffs. Would I be hung from the ceiling? My right hand had lost all feeling. Although the handcuff had been removed, my hand remained frozen in the same position on my back. Then it slowly responded to the pull of gravity and descended. I felt the blood rushing as though from an open faucet, down my shoulder and into my arms, and felt slightly better.

– Come.

Even the soles of my feet were numb. I kept walking. My feet felt like they did not belong to me. I had the sensation they were made out of burlap.

– Turn around.

Again, my back was to the wall.

– Sit down.

I could see from the chink in my blindfold that a blanket had been unfurled along the wall. I was made to sit down. It was slightly curled up under me. I could make out stains of blood and signs of vomit on the blanket. I sat down.

– Stretch your legs.

I stretched out. The time of self-determination was over. I was to obey orders from then on. The handcuffs were still hanging from my right wrist.

– You. Give me your right hand.

For the first time there I felt connected to another human being; human warmth radiated from whomever was on my right side. The guard cuffed my right hand to this other person's left. My left hand was still free. My torso curved against the wall like a cane under too much weight. Could this luxury continue? Then I heard the rattling of handcuffs.

– Give me your left hand.

My optimism faded. Where was he going to tie my left hand? He raised my hand to the bars of a window above, and snapped the handcuff shut. I remained crucified to the window by one hand, but this was a much more comfortable position compared to what I had endured – almost paradise! The blindfold started to fall from my eyes and I feared this would unleash another torrent of abuse, so I asked the guard to fix it. Over the last few seconds I had moved more than I had during the previous three-quarters of the day. I had not finished my request when the blindfold started to slip, little by little, down my nose. My eyes were tearful at the shock of seeing the faded light in the cell. I saw the tired face of the guard. He was drenched in sweat, as if he had just stepped out of the shower. What could he have been doing at that hour to cause such perspiration? In that fleeting moment I saw his sallow, murky face, long nose and narrow eyes. I could not tell what color his eyes were. But I saw his red and green sash,[1] soaked in blood.

– Why did they bring you here?

– I don't know.

– Then why didn't they bring my father?

An elegant ridicule, as well as a solid factual question! It was impossible for him to even imagine an innocent person being locked up here by mistake. But why did he single me out? Maybe I was only a suspect; maybe the case against me had not been made yet.

– *Oh, sweetie, take care, take care …!*

The gentle song filled the cold, empty space. Its sorrowful words were at once trite and primal. I had to move a little to feel comfortable in my sitting position.

– Aiiieee!

The person to whom I was tied let out a cry of pain. How could I inflict such pain with such a small movement? He appealed to me almost apologetically, in a whispering voice:

– Brother. Please. Watch my injured hand.

From my triangle of vision I saw what I would not have believed otherwise. The flesh had been battered around his wrist; actually, it had been cut open, as if a sharp knife had sliced around it. The blood had clotted around the circular wound. The handcuffs had cut deeply into the flesh. Had the blood not withdrawn to reveal the handcuffs, one would have taken the wound as a natural swelling on the wrist. The terrible crescent silver gleam of the handcuffs, however, left no doubt.

---

1. The officer in charge usually wore such a sash.

I started to economize my movements, especially those in my right hand. I even tried to move my hand according to his wishes. Probably he had been hanged from the ceiling. From the effect of the handcuffs on his wrists I guessed he was heavy. I looked at his hand and saw I was right. His palm was full, and his plump fingers were covered with coal-black hair. His fingernails were carefully clipped, which meant he had not been here long. The ridiculously selfish thought occurred to me that I was lucky to be relatively thin. Then I remembered how I had suffered just because my hands were tied behind my back.

– My *spirit, how sweet you are.*

Have you returned to the house, darling, or are you still pacing the streets, asking the scoundrels for information about your lost husband? Your husband went out to build you a house, to rid you of the agony of living in rented houses. Are you still weeping? May God protect you and bless your weeping eyes. When shall you ever rest? How and when did you sleep, my love?

An amazing calm descended on me, and I felt an ineffable comfort and ease during the rest of the night. Had it not been for the moans of my neighbor, I would have slept deeply and solidly until morning. But he kept me up. I finally figured out that my involuntary movements during sleep were the cause of his discomfort.

So here is a dirge to you, my friend, whom I knew not, nor ever saw. We spent half a night together in chains. I guess you did not live to spend many more nights. I hope you will accept my apologies for the pain that I caused you at the end of your short life. You do not need my pity, no matter how much I feel it.

Situations like this one reveal the strangest things about human nature. While I was tormented by the fact that my hands were tied behind my back, I could not think of anything but the immense pleasure that release from this bind would bring me.

But since my hand had been untied I could think of only one thing: hunger. I knew I could still withstand the torments but I did not know the limits of my endurance.

The sandy glass of the dawn had broken, and its shy light spread. The jingle of keys turning in locks and the creaking of iron doors was enough to cause new apprehension in the frightened inmates who awaited the unknown. A swaggering guard, against sounds of kicks and punches, called the names and barked orders.

– Yallah! … Faster! … Get that chamber-pot out of here! … Come on, faster! …

Blows and the filthiest of gutter insults were used as wake-up calls. Where were they taking them? Maybe to the toilet. But there was a mention of chamber pots. I had not known there were any. Finally I smelled the aroma of hot bread and eggs; my mouth watered. I wondered when our turn would come. The ogre of hunger was loose. Someone asked:

– And what about this crowd in the vestibule? Have they been dealt with?

Then someone was thinking about us. All my senses were sharpened. I automatically shook my left hand that was locked to the window. It was numb. No one answered the question.

– Anyone whose name is called must step forward and produce his own blindfold.

This did not concern me, as I was already blindfolded. They had forgotten about feeding us. We had not been dealt with.

– Agheel Abdullah … Kothayer Ahmad … Hussein Abd-e Ali …

I got to ten and then lost count.

– Mustafa Ali Othman.

I responded to this jumbled version of my name by rising automatically. In doing so I pulled on the hand of my friend in cuffs and caused him to shriek; I cursed myself for my thoughtlessness. One more name was called:

– Waheed Taleb!

– Here.

My handcuffs were finally unlocked. Somebody pushed on my arm:

– Get going.

My right hand was completely numb. I had no strength, and was being pushed along.

– Up the stairs. Fast.

I went up a few steps and was directed to turn right and then around. The cold, humid air on my face caused me to shiver.

– Stop here.

I stopped.

– Give me your hands.

Thus I was being handcuffed again. I put my hands behind my back.

– Not from behind.

I could not believe my good fortune: finally liberated from the modern method! From then on I was cuffed according to the national tradition. Another loud voice, which reminded me of my arresting officer, boomed:

– Where are these dogs?

The murmur inside the dungeon resumed.

– What the hell happened to their blindfolds?

– ...

– Tear their clothes and tie their eyes. They won't be needing them any more.

What was the meaning of this? It could have but one: impending death.

– You sons of whores! Stand here. Agheel Abdullah. Kuthyer ...

We appeared to be boarding a truck. My name was the one before the last. In order to get on the truck I had to pass by the man reading the names. I decided to make the best of this opportunity.

– They have made a mistake about my name. You called me 'Mustafa Ali Othman'. My name is Mustafa Ali *Noman*!

– Same difference. Get on.

His tone was harsh. I gave up and got on, followed by the man they had called 'Waheed'. He sat next to me at the end of the wooden bench that extended on three sides of the truck. I had seen his face from the opening in my blindfold when he was being pushed up the ladder. He was about twenty-five and good-looking. Old-fashioned, large gold rings adorned his fingers. The guards left, and we could hear the distant hum of their conversation. I asked Waheed:

– Where are they taking us?

– Probably to Emarah … Basra is full. It cannot hold any more prisoners.

He was quiet for a while and then said:

– What can I tell you? I don't know. These who are traveling with us are condemned to death. They will be executed in Baghdad.

A reproachful voice was heard from outside the truck:

– You are here, and the door is still open!

A quick repentant inhalation was heard, followed by the footsteps of someone getting on the truck. Two guards were posted by the enclosure at the back of the truck. They were separated from us by iron bars. Then someone locked the second iron gate that enclosed the entire truck, leaving the guards in a prison of their own. They were sitting on thick blankets and their faces were wrapped in black *yashmaks*.[1]

_____

1. A *yashmak* is one of the names for the familiar headdress worn by most Arab men.

As soon as the truck started its sluggish progress a blustery polar wind started to roar in. I buttoned up my summer jacket and turned up its collar. The truck was covered, but there were enough chinks to allow the cold wind to penetrate. I tried my best to take in the last scenes of freedom, but could not make out any of the streets and buildings of Basra. As the sound of cars was quieting I guessed that we had reached the suburbs. We were leaving behind all we loved and longed for.

With the shaking and rocking of the truck I heard the snoring of one of the guards while the other started to sing a boring tune in a bad voice. I guessed he was trying to turn back the tide of drowsiness that finally got the better of him. I rose my head with extreme care to direct the triangle of vision toward him. Hugging his automatic weapon and wrapped in several blankets, he was fast asleep.

On my right side a boy not much older than my own son was clutching a striped blanket and a threadbare towel. The care he lavished on them suggested that they were the only things he owned. He embraced these the way a child holds his favorite toys. We were both shivering. I whispered:

– If you let go of the blanket, we can wrap it around and we will both be warm.

But he just pushed the covers harder to his bosom as though afraid he would be punished if anything happened to them. I thought about him and the other three children in the truck. What could they have done so terrible as to warrant the rape of their innocence? I repeated myself. Again, he pretended not to hear me. Despite his tender age, he looked gloomy and defeated, crushed under the weight of a force beyond his ken. Probably the man sitting on the other side of him heard my request, because he whispered something in the boy's ear – whereupon he relented and shared his blanket. I helped him unfurl the blanket and even managed to offer Waheed a corner of it. He whispered his thanks to me in a voice trembling with gratitude. I started to feel a bit of warmth, which was what I had been dreaming of since boarding the truck.

My blindfold had slipped due to the shaking of the truck. Since my hands were tied in front of me, I could stabilize it; but I used the opportunity to look at what remained of the covered faces of my fellow travelers. At the end of the opposite row sat a young, handsome man of about twenty-four leaning on the divider between the soldiers and us. His moonlit, pale face featured a downy moustache.

– Why did you give them my name, Nomeir? You know I had nothing to do with these things.

I eavesdropped. The child answered:

– What could I do? They were going to kill me under torture. They asked me for a name. I gave Father's name but they said that did not count. So I gave them yours.

– But I am your uncle.

– They were about to kill me, as they killed Haleem right in front of me.

The uncle repeated:

– But I know nothing about the 'manifestos'.

– Neither do I. We found them in our desks at school. They did not believe any of us.

– Do you know that they are going to execute us?

– I know … but who told them?

– Shut up, you faggots!

The sentry had probably got his share of sleep as he followed his order with a hard blow to the bars with the butt of his weapon. I felt intimidated and lowered my head. The solid, imperturbable impression of the young man in the opposite row, however, was unchanged. He reminded me of the rock face of mountains. His was defying death. But I was shaking with dread and cold.

The truck stopped at one in the afternoon. I guessed we were near Sheikh Saad.[1] The aroma of food was tearing at me. One of the guards got off, locking the second gate of the truck behind him. Time had lost its meaning or we had lost the ability to feel its passage. The outer gate of the truck was opened and I expected that we would soon continue our journey. But then the second gate clanked open. Had we arrived?

– Here … Here …

We each received an orange. I peeled mine with trembling fingers. It occurred to me not to discard the skin, and ended up devouring the pungent peel that burned my tongue. I washed it down with what was left of the orange. This only served to awaken the sleeping monster of hunger. Was this orange our lunch? Maybe they were thinking it was pointless to feed us as we were going to die anyway.

Night fell. The slow progress of the truck grated on our frazzled nerves and used up what little remained of our endurance. When the light was dappling the treetops I could guess our whereabouts by looking up through occasional chinks in the cover of the truck. At night the only light came from my neighbor Waheed.

---

1. About 110 miles south of Baghdad.

Baghdad, Belly of the Beast

Waheed whispered:

— I have taken the blindfold off my eyes. We shall arrive in Baghdad in a little while.

I did not dare follow suit. But I did lift my head to see that the sentries were amusing themselves by watching the cars that passed us. They imitated their infallibly fashionable leader by wearing red *yashmaks*, and in a similarly eccentric manner. Soon we could see the tops of Baghdad's streetlights. I lowered my head, and as I had expected Waheed to put his blindfold back on.

— Why were we in Baghdad? What is going to happen to us?

When the truck stopped, we could hear the strident footsteps of dozens of soldiers who ran towards us and surrounded the truck with a sense of urgency.

— Weapon parade …

— Ready …

Although I was mostly concerned with my own safety, my heart went out to the boy sitting next to me. He was folding his blanket with trembling hands; I did my best to help him. Then I remembered that they were probably headed for the gallows and a flood of shame washed over me.

— Agheel Abdellah!

I especially remembered the name of this Agheel whose name started the roll call. I wished to see him at least once before he perished at the hands of the executioner. I wished I could help carry his coffin, attend his wake and say a prayer at his graveside if the regime would allow him such luxuries. I remembered that Jawaad Kazem's widow of had been warned against four activities upon receiving her husband's body: no wake, no public burial, no wailing and no wearing of black.

The trembling of the child next to me had turned into convulsions. His knee was hammering my upper shin. I had a desire to hug and comfort him; I saw my own Abeer and Ammar. Despite having given up the belief in miracles long ago, I wished for one right now to save him and my fellow travelers from death.

One of the sentries was posted at the inner door of the truck to deliver those of us whose names were read. More than one person seemed to pull and push the prisoners who were called off the truck. They would be lowered from truck and loaded onto what appeared to be a car. Six names were called. Then we heard the sound of a car turning on and speeding away.

– Mustafa Ali!

I stood, and no one pushed me. As I got off the truck the hand of a soldier pulled at my handcuffs to keep me from falling off the ladder.

– Give me your hands.

The handcuffs were unfastened. But I kept my hands together, waiting for orders. I was freezing.

– Take the blindfold off your eyes.

Thus the main interrogation began. But why in Baghdad? I raised my hands to my blindfold and took it off. I saw two handsome young men in front of me. One was wearing a light suit that was not appropriate for the season. I did not see much of the other as he was standing in front of a source of light. We stood in a huge yard covered with asphalt and cement. I was bent over due to the cold and also because I needed to relieve myself. I begged:

– May I be allowed to use the toilet? I have spent thirty-four hours without food, water or relief.

I said this and turned my eyes away, fearing a degrading response. But I heard a voice that at once asked a question and answered it:

– Can you run? Come on then; run.

He took my hand and pulled me. As we began to jog, I thought I was not going to make it due to cramps, exhaustion and extreme hunger. After about five minutes of this we entered the narrow doorway of a one-story building lit by a weak, sallow bulb.

– The toilet's to the right.

When I was finished, I was brought to a room with Waheed. The officer was looking at some papers. He noticed how Waheed and I were shivering and silently pointed to a kerosene burner. We sat on two chairs near the burner. I felt pleasantly warm and safe, and so did not dare question the officer about the reason for my arrest. I did not want to appear to be exploiting his kindness. When the officer left the room, Waheed asked:

– How long do you think we will stay here?

I motioned him to be silent lest the room be bugged. It was past seven o'clock and the heavy silence made me think of my family. What had happened to them? Had they accepted the decree of fate, or did they still grab at straws of hope? The officer returned and faced Waheed, squatting:

– Is this your bag?

– Yes.

The officer opened it.

– Look at it. Are these all its contents?

– Yes.

The officer rose. Gold rings sparkled on his fingers.

– Lock it and take the key with you.

Waheed put the key in his pocket. The officer stared at us. His black, combed hair was streaked with silver. From his calm, unlined face no one would guess his filthy occupation. Was it possible he was simply a good man who had somehow ended up in the wrong line of work?

– You may be in time for dinner.

He presented our papers to a young man and ordered him to be quick. We were brought to another three-story building. I was so tired that going up a few stairs made me gasp for air. On the third floor two sentries holding their weapons against their shoulders took over. They took our papers and sealed them. There was a wide passage with iron doors on one side and regular ones on the other. One of the iron doors opened, and we entered a passageway with small cells on each side. It looked as though no more than two people could fit in each cell. After twelve steps we reached a wall of thick iron bars with a door in the middle of it. A group of men wearing pyjamas and *dishdashehs*[1] crowded on the other side.

We were searched before entering the cell. A pack of licorice gum was discovered on me. I had completely forgotten about it. When I protested its impending confiscation, the guard tore off a sheet containing ten pieces and gave it to me. I felt like I had won a small battle. Then he yelled:

– Where is the section leader?

A big, white, young inmate, who seemed in good health, suddenly appeared.

– Yes sir?

– Where would you put these two?

---

1. A *dishdasheh* is a white caftan customarily worn by Arabs.

He answered with the kind of alacrity that corresponded to his sudden appearance. His accent betrayed Kurdish origins.

– In Number Twelve.

He locked the door behind us and I followed him, cowering with fear. Then he motioned to me.

– Here.

We walked through a passageway. The space on either side of the corridor was subdivided with metal partitions into eleven cubicles. In each cubicle one could see what was happening in the one directly across it. We walked to the end and entered a collective cell. We had hardly sat down when a torrent of questions rained upon us, as though we were extraterrestrials who had just landed on Earth:

– What is your charge? What have you done? Do you know if your case is serious? What do you do for a living?

My first guess was that there were ten inmates to a cell. I did the sums: 110 inmates in total. The following day I discovered that I had underestimated the number. Each cell, six by eight feet, contained fifteen to eighteen men. Yet despite the exhaustion, restraints and reduction of my humanity to the banality of a mere number, I found myself in a space suffused with human warmth. These men might have violated the laws of society or they might have been criminals from the point of view of the state, but I believed in their innocence partly because I knew my own and partly because they received me with open arms; I felt I was one of them. This conferred upon me the privilege of asking a favor.

– I am hungry. I have eaten only an orange with its skin in the last thirty-four hours.

– Here! Fish, bread. Do you want a biscuit?

What bliss! Three sardine-sized, boiled fishes covered with frozen grease, dry bread, an onion and three strands of parsley. But it was real food, and an absolute delight to eat after such a long fast. I felt like I was in the cheapest restaurant in the world, but I enjoyed that meal more than any I had ever had.

I thought of my wife. The first night of my absence must have lasted an eternity for her. I remembered that once I had been delayed by the unexpected visit of inspectors from the ministry of education, headed by the deputy minister. He was an ugly and pompous man who parroted a string of platitudes at great length. I returned an hour and half late to find my wife at the intersection. She had tied her hair with a kerchief that was soaked with tears. How did she spend the last night, the ensuing day and now this second night? How had she coped? Despite pondering the enormity of the disaster that had befallen us, I could not stop eating.

As soon as I took the first bite the dam of formalities broke. It was as though everyone were saying: 'You asked for food and got it. Now eat and don't be so formal'.

– Hey, why did they bring you here? Where are you from? Do you know how lucky you are?

That last comment struck me as odd.

– Lucky?

– Because you are here!

Many nodded in agreement as the circle around me grew wider. This gave me a strange feeling of self-importance.

The second time was about six months earlier. My wife told me:

– Did you see the car parked up the street? Maybe they are watching us.

– Nonsense! What do we have worth watching? You are going senile at thirty-five!

– Don't be silly. I will tell you tonight.

But I forget to ask her about it that night. After a couple of days she repeated her suspicions. This time I yelled at her:

– Why don't you stop? Am I that important to be the subject of surveillance?

She responded in a whisper, fearing she would be heard by the children.

– Take the house of Abu Samir the carpenter. They executed their son. The father hid and his other sons ran away. Only the wife and small children remain. And what about Zeinab's brother Jafar, who received a ten-year sentence? The only two houses unaffected are Jawaad Kazem's and ours.

In those days I used to buy a few beers on the black market and enjoy them pretending to be in the pre-Black February[1] years. I laughed:

– Come now, do you have to be so foreboding? Isn't it reasonable to assume that they are watching Jawaad and not us?

But after a couple of weeks her suspicions were confirmed. We were returning form an outing when we saw a green French car parked at our door containing two passengers. One was a portly young man in his early twenties who looked like the type of actor who appeared in food commercials. He had an easy-going manner about him. I was sure this was the first time I was seeing him. But I had seen his partner somewhere, although I did not know where. Maybe he was a neighbor. His hair was grey, and one would not call him neat; he had the appearance of a drunk, maybe because his smile looked fake. The interesting thing was that despite my terrible memory I somehow remembered his first name – Ramadan. I told my wife:

– I am sure they are at the wrong house. They must be looking for someone else.

We walked for a long time by the river, enjoying the view of the incoming tide and the fast boats that navigated the waves at al-Jazirah.[2]

---

1. The reference is to February 1963, when the Baath Party assumed power.
2. A beach north of Basra.

I greeted them, but they brazenly demanded to come in. I agreed but deliberately used a dry formal offer. I still expected them to transact some business related to the school. One of them asked:

— It is strange that you are not curious about our identity and purpose.

The drunk-looking guy laughed. I smiled tightly and said:

— You are welcome in my house, whomever you might be.

As I was bringing them cups of the lentil dish my wife had prepared, the younger agent dropped the bomb:

— We are from Security.

I almost lost control of myself. My mouth dried instantly. It took every effort not to drop the tray. My mind was racing with questions. But I knew that dropping any pebble in this pond would cause a wave that would not be favorable to me. So I remained silent.

— We have been watching your house for a few weeks now. We have also questioned all of your neighbors. Our conclusion is that we have to go with the best, so to speak.

I smiled, now on pins and needles. I knew that the drive to expand membership of the Baath Party was in full swing, using the water hose as an incentive. I feigned ignorance:

— I don't understand.

— You are required to fill out this questionnaire. A fine character like you must be a member of the Party. Such a solid and respectable citizen with an unassailable record must join and fight the good battle along with the rest of us.

The picture was clear enough. If I refused, a 'traffic accident' or some such could easily be arranged. My children would have to count on the generosity of a government that did not take pity on widows of political casualties — especially those with 'nationality' problems. The choice was between a dark destiny for my family and the appearance of a normal life that would be purchased by signing the deed of my own slavery.

The 'questionnaire' mentioned that I would have to agree to Article Seventeen of the provisional constitution indicating that, as a member of the party, I would forfeit my life should I ever assist any other group or party or hide relevant information. I signed, thinking of only one thing: leaving the country by any means and saving my kids from living in this cesspool. The agents left, gloating over their victory. My wife wailed:

– Didn't I tell you our house was under surveillance, man?

The humiliation of signing up in the party was more than I could take. I was just looked at my wife absently, stunned. She held me and whispered:

– Don't worry. We'll complete the house and sell it. We shall liberate our children and ourselves. We'll go away, wherever people are free.

Still, I remained silent. She kissed my forehead and continued:

– They tortured Khateeb Majidah for three straight days. Saleemah's cousin had to go into hiding. They burnt an army vehicle and blamed the son of my other cousin's neighbor and sentenced him to ten years in prison. Have you not heard stories like these? Have you not told me worse? Thank the Lord they have not kidnapped one of our children as they did to Ismail. Thank the Lord they did not hit one of us with a car, which is what they did to Umm Jaaber when she was returning home with groceries. Thank the Lord and keep your peace until we can escape!

Then she laughed bitterly and mocked my earlier words:

– 'Am I that important!' Now you know how important you really are. And tell me this: how would we escape without passports?

My memories were interrupted by one of the inmates:

– Are you daydreaming?

– He must be reliving what cannot be forgotten.

I returned to the present and asked:

– Why am I supposed to be lucky?

– My son … He who comes here is safe from death. This is the house of the living.

The speaker was an old man of more than seventy years, wearing a yellow winter *dishdasheh*. A man in his thirties laughed:

– Thank the Lord.

I swallowed my food and announced in a loud, sardonic tone:

– Lord, I offer my thanks, but I have no idea what the hell is going on.

One of them patted me on the shoulder and said:

– Soon you will understand everything. Don't be in such a hurry.

– Why did they bring you here?

– I don't know.

– Do you have a relative in the Soviet Union?

– No.

– How about in Bulgaria?

– No.

– Are you a goldsmith?

– No.

– Do you work in the movie business?

– No.

– What do you do for a living?

– I am a high school teacher.

– Is there any money missing at your school?

– No.

– Do you have a car?

– Yes.

One of them laughed triumphantly, as though he had discovered the crime of the century.

– Aha! Got it! Did the license plate fall off, by any chance?

– No.

– Is the deed in your name or in the name of the person who sold it to you?

– In my name.

I saw question marks on the faces of those around me. I had become a problem that could be solved only by some electronic brain. I was not aware that there were so many bizarre offences for which a man could be punished. Although I was still ravenously eating I had difficulty swallowing my food. My fellow inmates were asking me of definite things that they encountered in their lives and which caused them to suffer punishment. But I was not in their range. My charges were unknown and probably more dangerous than they could imagine. One of them stood up. I thought this was an act of despair but he called on the section leader:

– Faegh! Faegh! One moment please!

Faegh appeared.

– Yes?

He was well-shaven, and his white, glistening skin added to his authority. He started his interrogation:

– License plate?

– No.

– Terrorism?

– No.

He went through the probable causes of my arrest, which I had already rehearsed. He started to talk to himself and his Kurdish accent added an air of adventure to his monologue:

– If he were a Communist or a Khomeinist, or even accused of these offences, they would not bring him here. If it were a case of financial malfeasance, the investigation would not stop. So why did they stop? Did they interrogate you?

– No. They only asked my name.

– Did you travel to the North after May 11th?[1]

– Yes.

– What parts did you visit?

– Many places.

– Do you have friends among the rebels?

– The rebels?

– Yes.

– I am just a single, ordinary man.

One of them laughed:

– Which means you are singularly dangerous.

I smiled and finished my food, shaking my head. He added:

– Don't be puzzled. You will see. Everybody is dangerous. The only safe men are the dead and the prisoners.

– You are hiding something.

I looked at the one who had said this. He had a heavy moustache and a thick but well-shaven beard. His features were calm. Next to him sat a thin man with big eyes. This pair seemed better educated than the rest. The thin man replied to his friend:

– I think you are wrong. He is telling the truth.

To lend support to his estimation, I volunteered:

– My name is Mustafa Ali Noman, but they keep calling me Mustafa Ali Othman.

He puckered his lips in silence as everybody appeared to puzzle over the import of what I had said. One of them shook his head and put in:

– Even if you were mistaken for someone else suspected of associating with the rebels, you would still be considered too dangerous for here. The dangerous types are over there in solitary confinement.

He pointed to the cells that lined the the passageway on the other side of the iron bars. Another one added:

---

1. On May 11th 1970, the Kurdish rebellion under the leadership of Mullah Mustafa Barzani was brought to an end.

52

– Some of them are on death row and some are awaiting sentencing.

At this, I felt some tranquility.

– At least it appears that I will remain alive. A miracle has rescued me from the fangs of wolves. But how will my family know I am still alive?

Then I was told:

– Here is the shower.

I repeated the word without really believing my ears:

– 'Shower?'

Three faucets, two showers and soap. This was the lap of luxury compared to the dark dungeons of Basra.

On the way to the showers Waheed, my neighbor in the truck, greeted me. I saw his eyes for the first time. He had beautiful, light hazel eyes and wore an elegant khaki jacket. When he washed his face he appeared even more handsome. We embraced and kissed like long-lost friends. Living through twelve hours on that truck was enough to cement our friendship. He asked me:

– Is it true that you don't know what your charge is?

– Look into my eyes. Do you see a liar?

He laughed heartily. I asked, in turn:

– And you?

– I was exchanging foreign currency when I was arrested. Didn't you see my briefcase?

– Why didn't they prosecute you in Basra?

– They want to send me back to my hometown for sentencing. I believe there is some kind of a report on me there.

Waheed had worked in a foundry, and resided in a hotel where he got involved in currency exchange for migrant Egyptian workers coming from the Gulf states. He spent five days at the processing center for new detainees, where he found out that those who were traveling with us were on their way to be executed. Three of them were leftists and four were Islamic activists. I interjected:

– But there were seventeen of them.

He told me seven of them were political activists who had gotten into trouble. The rest did not belong to any groups. They had just been forced to confess under the kind of torture he shuddered to remember. Returning to his own case, he thanked God that some of those arrested were from his own neighborhood. He believed this was why he was not robbed of his money and jewelry at the jail. Of course, he did not credit their decency or solidarity, but the fact that many people had witnessed his arrest and knew what he'd had on him at the time.

I washed my socks. Fear for my safety ran parallel with anxiety for my family, but I slept with the feeling that my release was nigh. Our treatment there gave me the impression of being exposed to a breeze that brings rain clouds. They brought us two daily newspapers and a ration of four cigarettes for the smokers. The ration was yet more generous, as half of us did not smoke. Each cigarette was exchanged for five *fulus*. The guards brought us some clothes, which Faegh sold for them for a cut of the profits. Food was forbidden, as were alcohol and salt. (This last item was forbidden because not long before our arrival two death-row inmates threw salt in the eyes of a guard and disarmed him. They barricaded themselves and managed to dispatch four guards before being shot dead themselves.)

I was asked about fundamentalists in Basra, and whether it was true that they had entered into a coalition with the left. I replied that resistance to the regime continued, but thanks to the news blackout it was hard to divine the source of it.

I was in the section for 'detainees'.[1] The variety of people there was astounding. I met a couple of inmates who had owned

---

1. In Saddam Hussein's Iraq the word *mahjooz* was applied to anyone considered liable to break the law; thus, they could be held indefinitely.

and operated movie theatres; they had purchased films from a Lebanese distributor who turned out to have bribed some officials in the Ministry of Information to avoid taxes. The officers who had taken the bribes apparently got cold feet and blew the whistle. The distributor fled, but anyone who had done business with him was arrested. One of them, a large man in his fifties, told me:

– There is no law that allows the practice of detaining.

A professor of law, who was serving two years' detention, shot back:

– If there were such a law, you would not find anyone here.

The professor's crime was having said that 'someone' had monopolized the TV network to satisfy his narcissism, causing a rapid rise in the VCR and videotape market. He continued:

– Why detain people? If a crime is committed, there are laws to take care of it. I have never found anything like this in the constitution of a civilized nation. But 'someone' is a narcissist. He wants to force people to respect him, not knowing that they cannot respect someone who hides from them. Politicians usually say stupid things on TV. But this does not apply to him. He is the only politician whose very appearance on TV is a grand act of stupidity.

I tried to challenge him.

– Don't you think there is something personal in your hatred of him?

– Not at all. I respect him as an innovator. He has invented a thousand of ways to stroke his ego. He gives generously to the chroniclers of his gory autobiography. Then he makes sure that the book is turned into a trite and interminable movie whose first episode lasts an hour and a half. He has his portraits enlarged in London at exorbitant prices. He sponsors festivals of folk poetry to serenade him and praise his valor. The participants in the latest festival received stipends beginning at

1,500 *dinars*. There are music festivals to admire his supposed virtues as well. If the law is ever applied there will be no end to charges against him.

Two ranking bureaucrats were among us as well. They were rather aloof. One of them worked for the Revolutionary Parliament. He was detained because he could not account for the whereabouts of some important papers. The other worked for the foreign ministry and was arrested when some gifts that had been presented by foreign dignitaries went missing.

One of the detainees was an octogenarian who was senile and unable to speak or control his bodily functions. His son, who was also a detainee, took care of the old man's hygiene, gave him his pills and made his bed. The father had been in detention for two months on account of another of his sons, who was a student in Bulgaria. A member of the Baath Party had been murdered in a dispute with leftist organizations. As a result, all the students who were not members of the party were considered suspects. Since it was not possible to arrest the suspects, the government detained their parents instead. Although the head of the Iraqi leftist organization in Bulgaria was later assassinated in retaliation, hundreds of parents languished in prisons. The other son, who was an articulate and considerate young man of good education, was detained for a different reason. Of course he had denounced his brother to the interrogator as an ingrate and a renegade. But he had refused to disparage him in front of other parents, saying: 'I am against murdering people for political reasons and I am confident that my brother agrees with me on this. Therefore I think it unlikely that he has had any direct or indirect involvement in this assassination.' This was his crime.

Faegh, the section leader, came in to take down our needs. I asked for paper napkins, a pair of socks and underwear. I also bought a pair of pyjamas from an inmate. I wanted a different color, but he only had one kind to sell; I realized that his poor selection was responsible for my false impression that the inmates wore some kind of prison uniform.

My worries were turning into obsessive serial visions, but my thoughts regarding the car and the contractor remained terse and realistic: did my wife ever find the car? Did the contractor deny receiving the money? Otherwise I decided to ride my fantasies and let them take me where they would. This gave me the illusion of freedom, which was strange, because when I was free I would suppress my daydreams as they often depressed me.

Among us was a boy in his mid-teens from Karbala. He looked noble and handsome, but smoked a great deal. Everyone regarded him with compassion. His house had been raided, and as his brother had resisted arrest, all his family members were killed. He was saved only because he had been severely injured and presumed dead. He liked to show his scars from the five bullets he had received that day. He had spent eight months in detention.

At eleven o'clock all sections closed and the vice-warden, a tall man with dark features, came in to call the roll and grant such needs as extra blankets. When we prepared for bed I felt the pressure of packed bodies. One of the movie theatre owners and one of the shopkeepers donated a length each of their blankets for my sake. Yet the harsh, biting cold of Baghdad kept me up despite my exhaustion and sleeplessness.

At seven-thirty in the morning, eleven men were brought in. The youngest looked like he was in his mid-forties. They all wore yellowish khakis and marched as though on parade. It turned out they were municipal janitors caught drinking tea on duty instead of cleaning the street where an important person lived.

At nine an obviously retarded street vendor of foreign cigarettes was hauled in for overcharging. Next came a tall, blond man in expensive clothes, followed by a respectable middle-aged man with a thick, well-groomed moustache; then a heavyset, elegant-looking youth was brought in. For some reason people surrounded the youth like they had me. He revealed that he had been arrested because of his brother, an engineer in Denmark who had refused to come home to 'contribute to the nation's development'. Someone asked if this meant Iraq no longer had diplomatic relations with other nations.

The guards called for Ali Mohsen. He was a math teacher who had spent months in jail because of attending a party where politics had been discussed. Ali Mohsen jumped to his feet and ran towards the main gate, where he was told to retrieve his personal effects: it looked like his release was imminent. He started to dance and cry at the same time. Then he hugged and kissed everyone, and wished me luck in obtaining an early release. The two hotshot bureaucrats cornered him and began whispering in his ear, shaking their heads as if to emphasize a point. He waited for them to finish, with some impatience, and at once sprinted to the gate and squatted there. His friend asked him to return to his place until they opened the door. He responded in a comic, booming voice:

– Never! I shall defy the sting of lances before I forsake my position!

So Ali Mohsen departed, followed by many a wistful glance and fantasies of freedom. I, too, had been thinking similar thoughts. I went and sat in his vacated place. A man with a big smile knowingly tapped me on the shoulder and tried to soothe my melancholy mood with stories of his youthful adventures.

At ten I went to the infirmary to see a doctor about my foot, which had broken out in a rash. I was hoping to see the denizens of death row in their solitary cells; I had heard that they belonged to 'the resistance', which had shaken the ground under the Narcissist and his henchmen. Some of them had been discovered in urban safe houses and others were taken captive after being injured in battles. They would be rapidly dispatched unless suspected of having valuable information. I saw only two of dozens, buried alive in small catacombs. One of them had covered his head with a *yashmak*, and I could only see the yellowed whites of his eyes. The other had turned his back to the passageway. How I wished I could read their lonely thoughts.

– Mustafa Ali Othman with his personal effects!

I became excited at hearing my name. The inmates gathered around me once more, this time to congratulate me and ask me for favors once I was released and out of Baghdad. The two bureaucrats gave me their telephone numbers and then others came, each with his own request. What computer could remember all these chores? A crowd saw me off to the main gate. The bureaucrat from the foreign ministry whispered his telephone number in my ear again. The guard came for me and I left, holding a red nylon bag containing my personal items. I presently forgot all the chores I was entrusted with, and could only think of going back to my wife and Ammar and Abeer. I would take a long vacation, stay home and get thoroughly bored.

I entered a round room lit by the yellow and fading light of the evening. A well-built officer dominated the space. I remembered him as the officer who had processed me the day before. I felt I had entered the room during some kind of hiatus. My guard politely invited me to sit, and left. I sat near the kerosene heater. My head was racing with thoughts. He'd said 'please', so I had been proven innocent. Of course, he was frowning when he said it, but the security people are not in the entertainment business. They always frown. He said 'please', and the heater is actually a gas heater. This was treatment fit for a king.

The officer barked:

– Get a hold of yourself, you dog!

Shaken, I turned to my right and saw the respectable man with the neat, heavy moustache whom I had seen the previous day. He was leaning against the wall near the door. Heavens! What had they done to him? His face was battered, and he was shedding copious, silent tears. With his grey hair he was the archetype of a broken man. I trembled and tried not to look at him. On the wall opposite my seat hung a picture of the Narcissist, along with his words of advice to the security forces. The sanctity of the people and the necessity of their respectful and straightforward treatment were mentioned. I remembered the words of my friend Abu Waeel that the Narcissist was the head of the torturers in Karak.

My guard returned.

– Sir! Let's go.

I rose and followed him. I saw Ali Mohsen sitting in another room, holding three pieces of paper. His eyes shone upon seeing me, signifying a silent congratulation. We entered the room across the passageway. It was crammed with filing cabinets and metal desks. The only way to enter was sideways. I sat on a leather chair near the entrance. This position allowed me to see into the officer's room and most of the passageway. A nervous young man in his mid-twenties with fearsome teeth was at one of the desks in the room, speaking to a mean-looking colleague. But the guard who accompanied me was easygoing and pleasant. I was suspicious of his good disposition; I did not trust him. Even his smile looked booby-trapped. I was unable to read the ugly thoughts of this bunch in their faces. There was a time when our Bedouin ancestors allowed their thoughts to play out on their weathered faces and limpid eyes. There was a time when eyes revealed what was in the heart.

– Here are your papers. We will leave once you fill these out.

I did not dare ask where we were going. I could hear a continuing interrogation and beating of a man who'd had had a scuffle with a security agent:

– How dare you raise your hand to an *amin*![1]

The man lost his balance and fell back in the vestibule between the room and the passageway where I could see him. I thought he had assaulted someone named Amin; I soon realized my mistake and marveled at the irony of calling henchmen by that appellation. Blood was pouring from his teeth, on his lips and chin. The interrogator must have been a boxer. Another man whom I could not see had joined the beating. We were next to the station of the officer who had greeted us the day before, and whom I had thought a good man.

The man with the savage face and scary teeth called out:

– Abbas! Abbas!

– Yes, sir?

Abbas was a very short man with a white face and yellowish hair. His eyes were light hazel and he appeared to be a droll character. Yet I felt disgusted by him. He seemed capable of drinking human blood.

– Are you finished with him?

– Yes.

– It is not enough.

– Very well, then.

Abbas left and the interrogation resumed.

– How dare you beat an *amin*!

– But he beat me first!

– And what of it?!

1. *Amin* is both a proper name and a word meaning 'honest'. It comes from the same root that gives us *amanah*, which means 'security' in general and 'secret police' in particular. Calling a security agent *amin* is eccentric, but correct.

– I told him he could not leave before the end of the film! These are your own instructions! We are told not to allow anyone to leave the cinema before the end of the film. What if he was a terrorist who planted a bomb? The least we can do is force him to die along with his victims …

– But he told you he was an *amin*.

– He did not show me an identity card.

– So you are accusing a security agent of lying? Is it possible that an *amin* could lie?

– But he beat me first!

– When he struck you, that should have been your clue that he was an *amin*; only security agents beat people. That is what they do. They must discharge their duties to the revolution.

He decked him again as the interrogation continued in the passageway. Blood started to flow from the nostrils of the victim. Abbas now wielded the kind of cable used in high-power electrical towers.

– Take him upstairs.

– Yes, sir.

He led the victim upstairs while swinging the cable like a midget shepherd taking the herd out to pasture. Shortly, screams and pleas for mercy filled the room. Then Abbas returned, sweating profusely and panting like a mule after climbing a steep slope. He wiped his brow and glistening face. Another young man entered the room with a piece of paper, seeking a signature. Judging from his hideously mismatched clothes, he must have been colorblind.

– Get up there and sock him one.

– But I am in a hurry. Major Hamdan sent me …

– Five minutes only.

– Fine. Will do.

– Everything is upstairs.

The interrogator called out to another man passing by.

– *Amin!*

The man stopped in his tracks.

– Don't leave before a couple of blows.

– But Omar is already beating him.

– Well, help him out!

– We looked into his case. He has no record as a leftist and he is presently a 'supporter' of the party.

– 'Supporter' doesn't mean shit. Investigate his relatives, and if you find any communists, then …

He clapped his hands in joyful anticipation. Then he noticed me and shouted at me with anger:

– Go to the other room, if you please! Abbas! Abbas!

Abbas came running.

– Yes, sir?

– Is this the room for visitors? How many times do I have to tell you?

His voice rang with anger because I had been the unwitting witness of his treatment of a prisoner. He pointed to another room at the end of the passageway. I looked in that direction, and my eyes met those of Ali Mohsen again. We both were afraid of having seen the terrible beating. The room in which Ali Mohsen sat was small and empty. I squatted near the door in silence. I was afraid of speaking to Ali Mohsen, and he appeared so nervous he was almost choking. Although I had put a few feet between myself and the scene of the terrible beatings, I heard everything and had only to raise my eyes to see all.

– Take him out.

The sound of footfalls approached, but I dared not look up. I heard the voice of the interrogator again.

– You will regret hitting a security agent. You will wish you were never born. We will open a file on you here, and if it turns out that any of your relatives were communists, we will skin you alive. You may not travel from now on, nor start a business, nor work for official or semi-official organizations …

– You, come with me sir.

The easygoing guard was clutching a few papers. I stood, thinking I was probably going to be released. I could hardly suppress a smile of relief and followed him, almost running so as to avoid exchanging looks with Ali Mohsen.

– Where to?

– Transport Depot.

Are you returning me to Basra from there?

– No. You are supposed to go to Dahouk.[1]

– Dahouk? But why Dahouk?

– I have my orders.

I was struck dumb. My mouth dried. I was dismayed and felt like I was freezing. Thousands of questions were spinning in my head. We exited the prison gate. Everything I saw appeared vitally new and important; I was like a child discovering the world. A man in his forties was smoking and enjoying the sun at the door. Everyone seemed to obey him with a combination of fear and respect. I could not guess who he was. The weather was clear and sunny but cold. Tall trees leaned to and fro in their enviably carefree way.

A Land Cruiser took my cheerful guard and me and through empty streets, and past children playing in streets lined with trees and newly built houses. They had built an entire city within a city for those who ran this slaughterhouse. The well-shaded streets ended at a gate. The guards raised the bar of the roadblock for us. The driver avoided the busy streets and within a quarter of an hour we stopped in front of a building that looked like an old police station. Barbed wire lined the sky on top of the walls.

---

1. Dahouk is a city located 500 miles north of Baghdad. Basra lies about the same distance south of Baghdad.

Purgatory: Transition to Mosul

A pot-bellied guard at the gate, who carried a ream of papers, was conversing with an armed guard. They were standing near a truck like the one that had brought me from Basra. His face was turned toward us, but I could not see his features. The guard at the gate was agitated. His voice was loud and he had a strange accent. My guard got out of the car, but received a rude welcome:

– I shall not accept a single inmate without complete paperwork. Understood?

My guard produced the papers. The gatekeeper signed and then smiled.

– We cannot have chaos here.

Then he moderated his tone further:

– One has responsibilities, you know.

I had a bad feeling about this. The guard bade me goodbye with his usual happy smile. The yard of the police compound we had entered was a huge rectangle with a length of more than sixty-five feet. There were metal doors on three sides of the yard, and the pleasant rays of the sun reflected from the fourth blank wall. A stone-faced sergeant took me across to a room at the opposite corner of the yard, following an imaginary line that connected the corners of the rectangle. The cold in the room was unbearable. It was a huge enclosure divided into a big room and two smaller ones. One was a dark room with two toilets overflowing with filth and a shower that was equally dirty and dingy. There was also a faucet one could see only after getting used to the darkness. But as good luck would have it, there was a small bar of soap there.

The smaller room was thirty feet by ten and featured a couple of sleeping mats, an old, threadbare pad and a good mattress lined with nylon at the bottom and covered by a couple of blankets. The ten denizens of the room gathered around me. The room was so big that even with these people it looked empty.

– Where to?

– Dahouk.

– Dahouk! Aren't you the lucky one!

– Why?

My heart leaped at the mention of luck again. I asked why they considered me lucky. They were joking, of course. I had just missed the car leaving for Mosul.[1] One of the inmates, who wore a policeman's uniform, said:

– They are going to Kirkuk via Dahouk.

– Yes. We are from Kirkuk.

– The car for Kirkuk left yesterday.

– How long does it take, normally, to Dahouk?

Somebody laughingly answered:

– Depends on Heaven's unaccounted favors! It could take from one to five days.

It was past two-thirty in the afternoon. An Arab[2] came in with a bucket of soup as another one, wearing a striped *dishdasheh*, served it. He had tied a kerchief to his head and appeared to know his business. The soup was poured into three

---

1. Dahouk is on the way to Mosul.
2. The term 'Arab' in all Arab countries usually refers to immigrant nationals of other Arab countries.

big bowls, and the attack started. Three people shared each bowl, thrusting cut pieces of thick, dry bread into it and proceeding to eat with their hands. There were pieces of chicken wings floating in the soup; I was famished, but the sight of three people sinking their fingers into the same bowl turned me off. There was another man who refused to join the feast, and he was sitting on the good mattress in a corner of the smaller room. I walked away.

Above each room there was an opening to the outside that let in a current of freezing air. Since the good bed was close to the opening, its owner had blocked it with a piece of cardboard from an old container of eggs. This device worked to some extent, but in any case the grave-faced man who had rigged it was not in much need of protection from the cold. He was wearing a thick *dishdasheh* topped with a thick sweater and jacket, and covered his head with a heavy, black *yashmak*.

I greeted him, breaking his wall of silence, and placed my nylon bag near his bed. But he offered me a place on his mattress and asked in the name of God that I accept his offer, which I did. He asked why I did not eat with the others. I just smiled and extended my arms as if to say: just so. He told me that kebabs were available at ten in the morning and four in the afternoon from the canteen, and that one could get a skewer for150 *fulus*.[1] He suggested I kill my appetite with bread and tea until four o'clock. I smiled.

– Great.

– You can also buy things like foreign cigarettes when they are plentiful on the market.

Every time the main gate opened and closed a new group was brought in and the same ritual questioning about origins and destinations was repeated. If the newcomers were to be sent in the same direction as some of the inmates, they would be

---

1. This price is several times above the regular price of the item.

welcomed into the fold of their future fellow travelers. The awareness of the difficulties of the trek melted formalities on the spot and generated warm friendships. This kind of instant trust was nothing short of miraculous in a society where the supposedly free people did not trust even members of their own families. I remembered Abu Waeel's words of wisdom: 'for the first time in human history the intelligence of children has become a liability, instead of a source of pride, for their parents.' I had laughed at this, as I understood his meaning. But a friend, whose son was only two, was puzzled. Abu Waeel explained:

– They have planted amateur spies in every household to the point where we are reduced to whispering political jokes even in our own homes. Remember the little girl who was the cause of her father's execution just because she answered a simple question at school? The question was whether her father loved the Leader, and she replied that she did not think so, because he spat every time the Leader appeared on TV …

Jail was like a Turkish bath where people shed their covers and let their hair down upon entering. Even members of the Party were seen as normal people despite their uniforms. I thought that probably jail suited me more than anyone else because trusting others was my natural inclination, and because I hated mendacity and duplicity. There is a *noble tradition*[1] to the effect that the true believer shall not be bitten twice exploring the same crack. But to my thinking, and this may be due to my flawed nature, it is better to be bitten fifty times exploring the same crack than lose faith in the humanity of a single human being.

– Please help yourself.

The grave-faced man offered me a cigarette, opened an empty container and placed it on the blanket as an ashtray. He was dark and brawny; his fingers were hard, and his hands were

---

1. 'Noble tradition' refers to a saying attributed to the Prophet Muhammad.

strong enough to snap a man's neck. Although he had only three more days to serve, his pessimism was as boundless as his physical strength appeared to be. He was not out of the woods yet. Nevertheless I congratulated him on his impending freedom, but that was before I learned his story.

A festering tribal animosity had taken political shape. His personal enemy from an opposing clan was an important party member at Amarah and headed a huge union. My interlocutor was a butcher who made a good living. He could not imagine how his rival had come by half a dozen witnesses to swear on the holy Qur'an and bear false witness that he had threatened his rival's life in his house and at the union. They also said that they had seen him set fire to his rival's motorcycle. The butcher's alibis, that placed him at his shop at the time of the incident, were not permitted as evidence.

– So, where is this freedom for which you are congratulating me? I am afraid he will use the same means that he used before, accusing me now of being a communist or a member of Da'wa.[1] He surely can marshal the false witnesses to 'prove' that I had asked them to join or to claim that I gave them party manifestos. That would be the end of me.

– Move, then. Go to another city and find work there. Be like a grass that bends with the storm.

– No use. He has sent word that he shall not rest until I am either a party member or dead. But I am certain that even if I sign up, I will still die at his hand. There is a bitter vendetta between our clans.

I was uneasy, and my head was swimming. He did not say anything for a while and then added:

– There is only one way out. I have thought about this long and hard.

– And what is it?

---

1. An outlawed Shi'ite political organization.

– I must kill him.

– Be reasonable. You will hang for it. There is joy in life, and you are still young!

My words sounded hollow even to me and I stopped. But I must say that I met few prisoners who were despondent like him. The eyes of most gleamed with hope. Actually, I was envious of their optimism. That glimmer of hope did not leave their eyes, even as they were on their way to the gallows.

Later that day I met a cheerful fellow whose right eye was bigger than his left. He was an entertaining speaker who had worked in Basra, Baghdad, Mosul, Kirkuk, Nasiriyah and Amarah, as well as in Saudi Arabia and Kuwait, as a strongman performer and jack-of-all-trades. There was not a profession in which he had not tried his hand, except perhaps working as a minister. He had been a blacksmith, writer, driver and adjutant to a commander. He had also been a thief, trafficked in alcohol in Saudi Arabia and Kuwait as well as running and using drugs. However, he told me:

– I was put in jail for a crime for which there is no punishment by law. I was going to Hillah by bus. There were sixteen passengers. Those behind me gathered their fares and passed them up to me. I added mine, and in turn tapped the guy in front of me to hand the money to the driver. He ignored me. I repeated my tapping and he got angry; he took it as an insult that he would be treated as the driver's assistant, cursed me and challenged me. Then he attempted to swing at me, and I returned his blow. He got the bus to stop near a garrison and had soldiers beat me to a pulp. He turned out to have been an agent of the army intelligence service, and a relative of the chief military judge to boot. Would you believe I received six months for a brawl?

The number of inmates kept increasing gradually, but at nighttime none had come in who was going my way. I was the

70

only one going to Dahouk. I bought a new shawl, as the cold was increasing by the minute. My fingers felt frozen and looked drained of blood. Walking was imperative to fight the cold and the temptation to fall asleep. But all the same, it was better than the first night I spent in the dark Security dungeon in Basra. Few were the ones upon whom fortune had smiled. They were those who had something like an old straw mat to use as a bed. But the only ones who really inspired envy were those being transferred to other prisons. At least they would not have to spend polar nights in this frozen hell. I would never have believed even a prophet if he had told me I would one day envy a prisoner for a transfer.

A few people were gathered in a big room, leaning on cold walls, buttoning up their jackets, wrapping their heads in their hands, hoping to flatter the demon of sleep. Some were starting to huddle together and form living shapes where they found pieces of cardboard. But I remained awake and pondered the idea of standing all night. After all I had spent a night worse than this. At least I could walk here. The drug trafficker implored me to use his modest bed, which was but a worn-out straw mat and a thin woollen spread. But the butcher from Amarah had me as a guest on his bed, and I ended up fighting the cold night by his side.

At ten in the morning I bade him farewell. I was astonished by his power, expressed in his alacrity and ease of movement. He effortlessly gathered his bed in a nylon cover and tied it with ropes, packed all of his belongings with speed and efficiency, and swiftly crossed the 150 feet that separated him from his transport. He walked as if he was carrying nothing heavier than a small pillow. Before leaving he hugged me and wished me a speedy return to my wife and children. His words came from heart and affected me so much that I started to cry.

Many others came. I lost my trafficker friend around twelve-thirty. He looked into my face. His hair was thick and matted, and his windbreaker was dirty and covered with oily spots. He sighed heavily:

– Today I shall see my family. Your wish is my command. Is there anything I can do for you?

I knew how poor he was, because he never smoked a cigarette or drank a cup of tea unless he was treated to one. I told him I feared he did not have the bus fare, and added that I was prepared to give him the money. He refused indignantly, saying he would never take money from me. He insisted I give him the address or telephone number of my wife's workplace, but I refused. He might have been honest in prison, but he was involved in unsavory activities outside, and my wife would be at her rope's end. Nevertheless, he gave me his threadbare woollen spread and thin straw mat; he had found those items right there. I would wrap the woollen spread around my head and lie down on the straw mat, which was literally coming undone. Finally I had something. Not much to write home about, but more than nothing.

The following day around noon, the metal door opened and seven people wearing nothing but hospital-patient uniforms – white cotton *dishdashehs* with green stripes – were hurled in. This shivering group just all sat down against a wall. Their necks were limp, and their heads lolled around. The group remained motionless and stuck together as though poured in plaster. First I tried to ignore them. The Arab in charge of the mess, an Egyptian, noticed I was trembling with fear and disgust. I finally gathered courage to look at one of them. He asked:

– What did you see?

– Their faces are wrinkled and they have lost all of their hair; I could see their oily hair follicles. Their eyes are dreamy and there is a great slowness in their movements. Their bodies are thin and they are not in command of their bodily functions, which explains the terrible stench.

The Egyptian shook his head.

– If only you knew what happened to them!

– Why? Do you know?

– Sure. We were sent to the infirmary together. I was with them but they did not do to me what they did to them.

– Are they lepers? Do they suffer from TB?

– No. Look at the one sitting at the end.

He was thin and tall, his head completely hairless.

– They brought him here for one day some six months ago. He was a prince among men and had thousands of *dinars* in his pockets. He was a blond, handsome man and his clothes alone constituted a fortune. Then they took him from here. I met him again in the asylum for the insane.

– And why the asylum?

– I don't know.

– Is he insane?

He chuckled.

– Not any more than I am. He used to speak just like you. He told anecdotes and made people laugh. I saw nothing but generosity from him. When he saw that the food was inedible he had it returned to the kitchen and treated everyone to kebabs from the canteen. It was a day to remember in the history of the Transport Depot. He remained here only one day. My Lord, what a kind man. He treated us all to tea and cigarettes and bought a case of soap for common use. After a week they transferred me to the infirmary because I had accused the police of stealing my passport, which caused them to label me mad. I saw him there again. They used to give him two injections every day. His health was clearly on the decline. I remained in the hospital for fifteen days, and by the last day he no longer recognized me. Even his features had changed, and his hair had started to fall. I have no idea what they gave him and why. God only knows.

– Were a lot of people in the infirmary being treated like him?

– Dozens. I heard that they were political prisoners, but they had not been charged. They did the same thing in Egypt to dissidents. One dies within a year of this treatment.

– But why not kill them?

He appeared puzzled for awhile, but then returned to his earlier recollections.

– Imagine! When he found out I was broke he asked me how much I wanted. I told him a couple of *dirhams*[1] to buy cigarettes. He gave me a pack of cigarettes and forty *dirhams*. One time he recognized me in the hospital and gave me ten *dinars*. But he was going mad. Finally he was unable to feed himself. He would just sit there and stare at his food for hours on end. A prince! A gentleman!

– And his relatives?

– This is exactly the point. They do this so their relatives won't even recognize them. They just sit there inert until they die. When there are no beds in the hospital they send them here, and when it is full here they are sent to Security. Then they return them here, and then to the hospital. They are on a vicious circle to the death.

Was the Egyptian telling the truth, or was this all a figment of his imagination? I approached the 'prince'. His hairless head looked like a rotten cantaloupe. I did not see his eyes because he was hanging his head between his forearms, and his sleeves covered them. But I could make out his protruding backbone from under his *dishdasheh*. He smelled as bad as the rest. I was nauseated and sad at once. Eight hundred years ago, a prince like this would fling gold pieces at panegyric poets who would sing his praises. But who would sing his praises here, except one

---

1. Twenty *dirhams* make a *dinar*.

poor, lost wayfarer? Even his relatives would not recognize him now, and if they did there was little they could do for him.

All I could wish for this sickly bunch of prisoners was a quick and painless death. After my encounter with them I have never been able to view human beings in the same light. For me humanity was a beautifully cut glass cup that fell that day on the ground and shattered into a thousand pieces.

I spent more than a week at the Transport Depot and observed hundreds of innocent people there. The most heartrending were the teenagers arrested for not carrying a birth certificate or draft card. They were awaiting return to their homes, having been exposed to the cold, insults and rape by the henchmen of the regime. The population of the Depot ebbed and flowed. It would suddenly explode with inmates to the point where one could not even walk. But the troubles of the crowd were more than offset by the entertainment it brought. It was impossible to be bored in the presence of many circles dedicated to magic, acrobatics, contests in arm wrestling, lying, exaggerations, cursing, folk tales, etc.

Toward the end of my stay I met a former legal investigator. He was younger than I, slightly overweight, and wore an elegant yellow *dishdasheh*. His hair was carefully combed and he carried the tribal insignia of the Abi al-Khaseeb. I was sure I had seen him somewhere before, but was unable to place him.

– Are you from Basra?

He smiled. He was on his way to freedom and awaiting transport to Basra. He had spent twenty days at the Secret Service jail and seen dozens of people who executed, including the minister of irrigation. He had graduated at the top of his class before being appointed legal investigator. At the slightest instigation he poured out many horrific stories, his eyewitness accounts as an inmate at the jail and then as an investigator.

He said he had seen a Special Forces sergeant who later died under torture; he had lost his mind after being forced to kill three children. Tranquilizers and injections could not blot out his terrible memories and guilt. In his uncontrollable fits of rage he would curse the Secret Service, his superiors and even the Leader.

– Only a few got away with their lives from that prison, and I am among them. One day they brought a man who seemed to be breathing his last. He said they had tried to force him to rape a man who was badly beaten, and he said he would not do that even if they killed him. He died a few nights later in his sleep.

Once, he continued, they had arrested the wife of an intelligence agent. At lunch, he told her how he had shot a five-year-old boy after they had raided a home and killed everyone in it. The child had run out in hysterics, and he felt that the best thing to do was to put the child out of his misery. After all, who would take care of him? His wife, who was unable to bear children and had listened in silence, overturned a plate of food on his head and left the house. At the police station she denied the whole story and promised to return to him, which she did. After a few days, the agent's body was discovered at the house, and she had disappeared in the impenetrable marshes south of Basra where she had relatives.

The stories ran on. The secret police had tapped the bedroom of an important state employee. His servant was bribed to replace the tape in the recorder every day. It turned out the employee was not spying, nor was he mixed up in any intrigues. But they still found damning evidence of a capital crime: he was called in to hear tapes of his amorous conversations with his wife; in the heat of passion, he had told her he 'preferred one of her pubic hairs to a hundred Aflaqs'.[1]

The legal investigator was in jail on charges of accepting the sum of twenty *dinars* as a bribe. That alleged amount was so

---

1. Michel Aflaq was the co-founder of the Baath Party.

paltry as to be ridiculous, and there was no evidence to substantiate the allegation. But everyone knew that there were always two charges: the overt charge and the real one. It was useless to challenge the overt charge, as that was only an excuse.

– My real offence was that I did not join the Party. They invented the bribery story to stain my good name and put me in jail. They had tried to bribe me with a judgeship, but I refused. They threatened my life, but I laughed at them. I told them I am not a political man and have no desire to be in any parties, but that if I ever considered joining one, I would choose a respectable one. My father was a nationalist, after all. Then they said they would dishonor me unless I joined their filthy gang. But they shall never buy my conscience! When the time comes I will be the first to fight them. As a nation we have sunk so low because they have been able to buy off all the cowards, opportunists and parasites. There is no one left unsullied except the truly noble. So they try to take away the only thing left them: their good name.

The investigator believed that a great deal of responsibility for the mass executions of the innocent was borne by the judges. For one thing, they were expected to call the accused in and ask questions in the absence of security agents. In fact they rarely did more than rubber-stamp confessions extracted under torture. But he had seen two exceptions. The first was a conscientious judge, a thorn in the side of the regime who had the wife of the mayor of Basra arrested for stabbing her cook. When he refused to bend to pressure and release her, they forced him to tender his resignation. That was a happy day for the Basra Secret Service. The other exception was a judge who imprisoned an interrogator who insisted on remaining behind when the judge wanted to clear the court for a private conference with a defendant who appeared to have been tortured. He also had broken a prostitution ring and arrested its leaders, who had Party connections. When orders for the release of the accused arrived from Baghdad, he resigned.

In my last days, I studied the walls of the Depot, which were covered with ugly graffiti indicating who had been there, when and where from. They were mostly dry and matter-of-fact, like so many entries in an attendance book. Maybe this triteness of expression reflected of the banality of life in jail. There were also a few squalid curse words. Among these writings, a couple of efforts stood out. One was written in beautiful Persian handwriting, featured the name 'Mahmoud Afghani' and was dated a year earlier. Why had he been there, in this graveyard for the living? I was still studying the walls when another Afghan was brought in. His name was Hossein Eghbali. He was a diminutive man with a yellow skullcap, green eyes and protruding oriental cheekbones.

He wept incessantly. Through a Kurdish cobbler who knew some Persian, we were able to understand enough of his Afghani dialect to piece together what had happened. He had been arrested near the Bab al-Kazem sanctuary for not having proper identity papers. He had left his family inside the sanctuary to buy milk for his infant daughter; his mother was sick and his father was an invalid. He carried all their money, and his father had the papers. As he did not speak Arabic he had been unable to communicate with the police. He was worried sick that his family would break apart without money and his presence.

Our enquiry was interrupted by the shrieks of another prisoner, a young man who had fits during which he would sob hysterically and scream that God was butchering his entire family with a knife, then abjectly implore God for mercy, run around and hide in corners. Finally he would utter terrible imprecations at God and other ghosts of his sick imagination. When he was calm, however, he used language only to formulate one question: 'Got a cigarette?' He was from around

Khaneghin,[1] and had witnessed the massacre of his entire family during the events of March 11th.[2]

At long last, I found a fellow traveler who was going part of the way to Mosul. Saber was a tinsmith in his forties. He had been under pressure to join the Party and inform on his neighbors at the bazaar who had leftist tendencies. He was then arrested on charges of not having served his reserve duties at Mosul. Now he was being sent there under arrest. He was afraid they might unearth his membership in the People's Army,[3] but I told him his fears were probably unfounded. All they wanted was to make him serve a bit longer and join the Party. But he said he would rather die than sign up. He was very sympathetic to the resistance and said that if he had seven sons he would give them all to fight the Baath.

Just before the end of my stint at the Transport Depot something extraordinary happened. The main gate of the prison opened and dozens of civilian men and women entered. We had been ordered to come out and meet our visitors while enjoying fresh air and sun. Why this consideration, why here and why now? I tried in vain to find one of the visitors to get word to my family that I was fine. But I got no cooperation, as fear makes people deaf and dumb. My Egyptian friend suggested we contact the relatives of Masoud, a very kind inmate. When we approached him, his mother and sister were hugging and kissing him and telling him how much he was missed. We kept waiting for a break in their outpouring of emotion to put my request, but the break never came. Soon we were called to go back inside and as my luck would have it, I had been last to exit the prison and first to have to return.

---

1. A Kurdish area in western Iraq near the Iranian border.
2. In 1970, government troops occupied the areas controlled by the Kurdish Peshmerga militias.
3. The enormously popular Abdulkarim Qassim, who was toppled by the Baath *coup d'etat*, had organized these units in 1958.

Soon afterwards, Saber and I were called to set off for Mosul. We rapidly said our farewells and left. Our companions in the truck were a homosexual from Sanjar, an army sergeant who had got drunk and picked a fight at a tavern and a timid and somewhat unbalanced youth. Soon we picked up four more passengers from Abi-Ghoreib. They seemed to have a leader, a roughneck missing a thumb on his right hand. The prisoners unfurled their spreads on the floor of the truck while Saber and I just covered our seats. The newcomers crawled under the blankets and engaged in horseplay of a rather lewd nature. The guard in charge screamed at them to shut up, but the roughneck peeked out from the blankets and yelled back:

– We won't shut up, and you'd better not raise your voice if you know what's good for you!

Incredibly, the guard did not respond and remained as silent as Saber and me. We arrived in Mosul at seven PM, three hours later than scheduled. The cold was unbearable and caused us to double up as soon as we got off the truck. The roughneck waved his arms to keep warm. It appeared that the warden was waiting for us although he could have gone home.

The building was about fifty years old. They had added a few rooms, the effect of which was like putting a new dress on an old hag. In one of the newly built, well-lit rooms sat a man in his thirties taking down names and separating the prisoners. Three tired old guards were lining up the inmates. The cold added a touch of agitation to their movements. They knocked on a metal door and a small aperture opened; after a short conversation between the guards, the prisoners were let in. The yard was rectangular, and the right wall was covered with hastily applied plaster of varying shades. The Sanjari youth and the timid young man were taken outside, where a car awaited them. After a few seconds the car drove away with the sound of screeching tires. There was no one left except for Saber and me. Saber had shrouded himself in a blanket. A stormy, arctic-caliber wind was blowing. He insisted that I take the other blanket but I refused, as I still had the old woolen spread. We waited our turn. The warden came out of his room and looked at me carefully. He asked about my profession, and appeared concerned. Finally he said:

– What is your charge?

– I don't know.

He interrogated me in the same manner as the prisoners had in Baghdad. I was astonished by his interest, but could not fathom his intentions. Something in the way in which he asked questions implied that he considered me a human being. I found that I admired him as a champion of humanity, despite his uniform.

– Sir! I wish to help you. Say what you want to say. Don't hold back.

I told him how I had been abducted, and that my wife and two children had no idea what had happened to me. I told him I wished to contact them. We did not have a telephone, but I could call the neighbors and leave word that I was alive and well.

He stood by the doorway and the pale light complemented his features. He had black soulful eyes and a deep voice. I felt I had known him a long time. I was seeing living proof that someone in his position could retain his humanity, that one had to avoid generalizations. He walked back from where he stood and motioned with his extended hand.

– Be my guest. Use the phone if you can. It has been out since the storm that downed the lines three days ago. But if you are still here when I am again on duty, I will help you call your family.

Saber and I parted in a warm mutual embrace. Neither one of us could hold back tears. His gloomy look said: 'You will never see me again.' Where would they take him? Where would they take *me*?

I was led to a door made of iron bars, into a narrow passageway and through a guardhouse to another metal door. Then I was made to enter a huge area, more than three hundred by one hundred and fifty feet divided on both sides by iron doors. A sergeant with a provincial accent barked:

– Choose a room and enter. At ten o'clock at night the doors will be locked.

I did not need to use the toilet, so I started peeking in rooms to choose one. The first was full of Kurds and Talarafis.[1] I tried another, and it was the same. In the third room I finally found some people whom I could understand, and was welcomed with the same warmth I had received in Baghdad. Dozens crowded around me, giving advice that included using the toilet before the doors closed. They brought me an orange, an apple and a sweet roll, but I was not hungry. I was peppered with questions about the situation in the south,[2] the Da'wa Party and the influence of Khomeini, and I told them what I knew.

They were all serving detention sentences of one month for the same silly crime: missing a license plate. That was the law; a missing plate meant a month in jail for the driver and two months' impounding for the vehicle. It was laughable, as two out of every ten cars in Basra were missing license plates. Why such zeal in enforcing the law here? There was only one explanation: the goal of the regime was to harass and to humiliate. There were no Shi'i insurgents or Kurdish rebels here to provide an excuse for mass arrests, but there were plenty of cars. There were fifty people in each cell, suffering away from their families

---

1. The Talfaris are a non-Arabic-speaking ethnic group living around Mosul.
2. Southern Iraq has a considerable Shi'ite population, which was the source of some resistance after the Islamic Revolution in Iran.

and losing income just because the license plates had fallen off their cars. How easy it was to send one's personal enemy to jail with pair of pliers and a few minutes alone with his car!

The fiftyish man to my right, who was being released the next day, was deliriously happy. The one on my left was being released in ten days. They were both extremely kind. But I was wary of a man in his mid-twenties. I had told the crowd around me that they could thank their lucky stars their cases were light, and reminded them that dozens of innocent people were being executed daily. The young man shot back:

– Whatever the Revolutionary Authority does is just!

I did not know if I should take him seriously. But his friend hit him on the side of the head:

– Shut up you stupid *thour*![1]

He then affected an exaggerated sneeze, which made everybody laugh.

– Am I a *thour*?

– Sure. Aren't you a '*thouri*'?

The room exploded with laughter again. Soon the inmates were preparing for sleep. They had buckets of fresh water, a chamber-pot and many nylon bags for rubbish. The warden's concerned eyes still regarded me. Why did he care so much? Because I had been sent across the country, without knowing what my charge was? Why did he ask me those questions? My papers must not contain a charge or else he would know. All they had on those papers was a mistaken name.

I considered giving my address to the guy being released the following day, so he could contact my family. But I was sure I would be sent away myself, because of the warden's tone. He had implied that it was unlikely I would still be there during his next shift. If I sent word from here my wife was sure to come

1. The speaker is playing on the similarity of the words *thour* ('bull') and *thourah* ('revolution'; *thouri* means 'revolutionary').

looking for me, and she was sure to be disappointed. I would probably get another chance at sending for them to come and see me. But who knew?

Around eleven-thirty at night I started to feel the pangs of acute dysentery. This was my worst nightmare: terrible cramps and diarrhea behind closed doors, among strangers. I sat up and tried to control myself for about half an hour. But the cramps and shooting pains were unbearable. My neighbor to the right woke up and asked what was wrong. I told him, and he directed me to use one of the garbage bags. I was dying of shame; I thanked God my fifty cellmates were asleep. Only one noticed me and turned around. But I knew this was just the beginning of the ordeal. At the peak of one of my attacks someone suggested I eat as many limes as possible. The attacks stopped at five in the morning, though I am not sure the limes had anything to do with it.

The fatigue of traveling by truck and sleeplessness due to dysentery had left me thoroughly exhausted. When they called my name at seven-thirty in the morning I could not feel my body; it felt like a bag full of straw.

A Land Cruiser took me to my new prison in the freezing cold. But I was not blindfolded this time. A glimmer of hope flashed in my mind as they took me through the inquiries office, which was warm and elegant. But I was soon processed and sent to a small building that appeared like an outhouse next to the main structure.

A sergeant opened the iron gate for me, and I went through another door into a passageway. The first thing I noticed was the thick cloud of smoke from cigarettes, which was unusual for this time of day. The passageway opened up to a number of tiny six-by-three-feet cells and there was a toilet and shower at the end of it.

The amazing thing was that each cell was crammed with thirteen to seventeen prisoners, though they could not have been meant for more than two inmates. The prisoners just sat next to each other along the wall, extending their feet across the width of the cell. The ceiling was made of cement and stood about six feet high. The humidity resulting from the breath of so many people formed as drops of water hanging from the low ceiling. These icy drops fell on the prisoners, as a maddeningly annoying slow rain. To deal with this problem someone had to get up every half-hour and wipe the ceiling dry with a rag. Of course this was not so easy, because the wiping volunteer would freeze his fingers in the process and had to warm up a couple of times before finishing the small surface. There was warm water once a week, which allowed a few people from each cell to bathe. But since I was the last to arrive my turn to use the shower never came.

After the rapid succession of events so far, this was the first prison to keep me for a relatively long time. There were three inmates in my cell who had been there longer than the rest. The oldest was a sixty-five year old Shabaki farmer named Sadoun, who was a bag of contradictions. He was illiterate but also wily in matters of culture, wealthy but stingy. His three sons had graduated from foreign universities at his personal expense. He had accomplished much in his life. I admired him as a man who chisels a statue from the rock face of a mountain. I asked why he had been imprisoned. He whispered his story:

– I am a well-to-do man from Shabakiah. My people are notorious for lack of culture and religious education. They are superstitious and given to bad habits like bearing false witness for money. I decided to help them by founding a *husayniya*[1] and bringing a cleric to rid them of base superstitions. We succeeded

_____

1. A Shi'ite congregational center.

to a great extent, but were forced to close it down, as it was viewed as a center for political agitation.

The second resident inmate was also a peasant, with large hazel eyes and a prominent beard, who was given the title of 'Mullah'.[1] He was theologian, politician and madman wrapped in one. No one knew why he was in jail. He busied himself sending epistles to world leaders like Carter, Sadat, Begin, Qadafi and Nkruma (the fact that the latter was dead did not appear to concern the Mullah). He called upon the world leaders to put an end to warfare and embrace the Soviet Union for the sake of world peace. When he started to talk he would not stop. I had often wondered about the fluid line that separates sanity from madness. I wondered how a man slips down the dark chambers of lunacy. Now I came face-to-face with a man who embodied the subject of those abstract thoughts. The first time I sat next to him I noticed he kept two plastic jars of different colors near him. One was for drinking and the other functioned as his chamber-pot. I had hardly sat down when he asked me his first question:

– Does your wife use birth control?

I was stunned. Was he joking? I had assumed that most everyone was asleep, but they were just numb. The Mullah's rash question caused someone to cry:

– This is his obsession! When will they take him away so we get a moment of rest?! Aren't our own troubles enough?!

The third resident of the cell was an apparently important trade union leader who had worked in a state-operated winery. He freely admitted that he had embezzled, but justified his actions: 'I could not manage my life on my salary.' He said he was arrested on a charge unrelated to his malfeasance.

I recall two other prisoners whose cases were similarly absurd. A young Mosuli man who was the procurer at a state-

---

1. A *mullah* is a Shi'i cleric.

operated chicken farm was imprisoned for saving money for the state. He had bought wholesale rather than retail, and had turned what he saved over to the treasury – his charge was engaging in black-market activities. He regretted his foolish honesty: had he just pocketed the money instead, he would have been a free and wealthy man. Another, who was only eighteen years old, had run afoul of the authorities on charges of nepotism. He worked in a cement factory, and was accused of putting his uncle ahead of others for buying rationed cement. He could see no rationale for the charges:

– Why don't they check his house? If he had cement he would have used it!

The rest of the inmates were charged with possession of firearms. There were forty of them in our section and hundreds more in other sections. Their leader was a gentle, and well-respected, fifty-six-year-old *sheikh* by the name of Mahmoud Zaher. He still acted with the magnanimity and poise of the tribal headman he was.

I never found out anything about the people in the other cells, but got to know the few who were kept in the passageway. There were three brothers who were detained because their youngest brother had refused to return from abroad. The oldest was a retired teacher and the second, a contractor. The youngest of the ones in jail was a pious doctor with a kind, bearded face. They were hopeful that they would be released soon, but this did not happen as long as I was there. They were transferred to the main prison, along with a wealthy Saudi whose uncles in Saudi Arabia owned what he described as 'half of the world'. He was a gambler who had lost a great deal at the Ghasr al-Abbasi casino in Baghdad and had been forced to sell his expensive car without first transferring the deed to the buyer. He was arrested at the gambling table while the car was still in the garage of the casino.

The other denizen of the passageway was a security agent. One of his kinsmen was an important member of the Party who had been executed for participating in an assassination attempt against the Leader. In his sorrow he had said enough to cause the end of his career and freedom. He had been sent to where he had relegated others. Lately he had come under the influence of the doctor and had taken to praying. But bending and prostrating in prayer had not dulled the spark of evil that still flickered in his eyes.

It was in this prison that I heard for the first time of the Ansar al-Islam guerrilla movement, from one of the peasants who was there for carrying arms. I asked about their chances and he said that the struggle was ongoing. His eyes were ablaze:

– They are hard as nails. They can never be defeated.

I was sure that once free he would join them in a heartbeat. The *sheikh* said he was also optimistic:

– As long as they carry guns, you can consider them victors.

The prospect of Ansar al-Islam's victory fired the peasants with such hopes that they would gloat over their would-be vanquished enemies.

Time passed very slowly, marked with heavy sighs, gnashing of teeth and bitter exclamations. At one point the youth from the cement factory cried out:

– God! You have created every species of animal and plant for a purpose. So what is the purpose of these hooligans?[1]

We had not expected this surprise ending to supplications to God. Everyone laughed, but this caused Sadoun's discomfiture. He shouted:

– How many times have I told you? Are you sure that this devil will not report you?

By 'this devil' he meant the former security agent in the passageway. Somebody replied:

---

1. That is, the Baath Party.

– Let him be. He is letting off steam. Besides, what more can they do to us?

The security agent grabbed the bars of the cell and said to the youth:

– Please! Repeat your prayer! I want to recite it after mine!

This time the trade union member from the winery took him to task.

– Listen, you! How did you rate your power and position when you were outside? Huh? Answer me!

The security agent thought for a while, smiling at the shut gate.

– Why do you ask?

– Just curious.

He appeared to remember lording it over people in the streets and within the organization. Then he shook his head with bitter regret and waved his hand above his head:

– High! Very high!

The trade union member, who seemed to remember his own authority, shot back:

– High? That is not high enough! Say you flew a few inches below God's throne!

This triggered the Mullah's indignant wail:

– Do not blaspheme! May God forgive us all!

Everyone laughed again. The trade union member, well wrapped in his red *yashmak* and sniveling from a bad cold, completed his thoughts:

– But now we are happy just to be alive …

A heavy silence ensued and every one of us withdrew into his shell. It was as if each was seeking a window to the past away from the surveillance of the authorities. We got used to waking up to the sound of the doctor's recitation of the Qur'an. His rich and compassionate voice reverberated within the thick walls and chased away the demon of sleep. I would just lie there, all ears, but the peasants would get up and make their ablutions in preparation for the morning prayers. This, however, happened only on the watch of a lenient guard known as 'Hajji' who was from a poor family in Mosul. But our other guard, who went by the name 'Sayyid', would not allow this. He had a thick moustache, oriental eyes, and, a mouth filthier than a cesspool which freely flowed to everyone except for Sadoun. I guessed that Sayyid was from the same area and knew Sadoun. This was our normal routine. But occasionally we were hit with another wave of prisoners.

Deluges of this kind would start with one person and increase exponentially until there was no place to sit. Then they would take scores of prisoners away and only a few of them would be left in each cell. No one knew where the prisoners were being taken and none dared ask. The waves would last between a couple of hours to half a day. But what we called the 'big wave' lasted for two days.

It started when a young, black-bearded, brown-suited medical student, no more than twenty years old, was brought in at eight in the evening. He sat between the Mullah and me. Fortunately for him the Mullah was still sulking over his last rebuke, or he would have bombarded the student with his idiotic chatter.

The student appeared deeply preoccupied. That morning he had been talking with a couple of friends at the university. One of them had wondered why the building was so clean, and the other replied that probably the Leader was scheduled to visit – or else they would not bother to clean up. The student had said: 'Isn't he afraid of being assassinated?' Then he had moderated this sentence, saying: 'It is necessary that such a visit be preceded by security precautions.' That was all he had said. Who had informed on them? He was sure it was not either of his friends. He was arrested within half an hour of this conversation and kept for eight hours in a room with two space heaters. This explained the fact that he was sweating profusely and smelled like he had not bathed or changed his clothes in a month.

The next morning a prisoner was brought in whom the student recognized as one of his three friends. Then the third friend entered around noon, and not long afterwards the student's two half-brothers were hauled in. One of them was a reserve soldier and the other was still in high school. Then his brother, father and cousin (who was a high-school teacher) joined the multitude. Before nightfall they brought fifteen more people, most of whom were medical students. By the third day our section hosted the entire cohort of the three students' adult male relatives.

The cell was so crowded that sleeping became impossible. We all had to spend the night standing. There were only thirty people in our cell, and we all tried to rest by leaning either on a wall or each other. The only one who remained sitting was Sheikh Mahmoud Zaher. We had him sit on a heap of blankets because he could not stand – he had developed a severe infection in his right foot. The stick had broken his right toe when the torturers were *bastinadoing*[1] him. He said the bone had broken through the skin, causing severe bleeding, but he had found it beneath his dignity to cry out in pain. This enraged his torturers, who then took up what they saw as a challenge to beat him until he cried. Fortunately, he had passed out before the prospect of dying under their blows became too real. They had thrown him out and had not bothered to call him back for more beatings.

Before the arrival of the medical student the *sheikh* had just wrapped his toe, which had swelled to the size of a small apple. The wrappings were awash in pus, and a mere touch would send him into paroxysms of pain. He had developed a fever and given

1. The *bastinado* is a form of torture that involves beating the soles of the feet with a stick.

up hope. The medical student confirmed a diagnosis of gangrene. The *sheikh* called one of his relatives from among the peasants to leave his last words regarding his obligations and property, which he whispered in a rapid, local dialect. When we lifted him to put him on top of the blankets, he looked at us with deep affection and said:

– I wish we could have met in a more proper setting.

Even speaking appeared to be painful for him. Before the onset of the infection he was a most affable and entertaining speaker. Someone had asked him about the tribal war between Shammar and El-Boumatiut.[1] He answered in the epic, oral style of the ancient Bedouin, prefacing each episode with: 'And thus says … , the son of …', or 'Thus says one of the *sheikhs* of Shammar, or a merchant from Mosul …' He had mentioned the 'virtues'[2] of each tribe, named the heads of clans from both sides and recited the battle cries for each engagement.

That night was very cold, despite the presence of so many bodies in a small space. One of the problems was a small opening to the outside. It would let in wind that chilled us right through, but closing it would have deprived us of the oxygen we needed to breathe. In either case the slow, freezing rain from the ceiling fell on our heads and shoulders. I slumbered a few times only to be woken up as a neighbor collapsed on me in his sleep. The luckiest among us were those who had something to wrap around their heads. But even they needed to wring their saturated rags several times.

Despite overcrowding, the prison was eerily silent. The reason was our new guard, who carried a machine gun and was in the habit of stepping among those sleeping in the passageway.

---

1. This tribal war was finally brought to an end in the traditional style, through the good offices of *sheikhs* from Saudi Arabia, Syria and Egypt, who negotiated peace.
2. The Bedouin tribes often recite qualities that make them superior to other tribes. These are known as tribal 'virtues'.

He would violently bang the bars of the cells with the butt of his gun if he heard a whisper. At that moment I became convinced that all or at least ninety-nine percent of the men in that prison were wrongly accused of sedition. If they were inclined to violence, they could have easily taken this lone, cruel guard hostage, or done him in.

Twenty-five hours after the beginning of the crisis, it came to a sudden conclusion. They transferred all the prisoners including some of our former fellow inmates, the chicken-factory procurer among them. He left me with a valuable piece of advice – if beaten, I should scream and pretend to faint:

– Don't play the hero for a bunch of lowlifes. Pretend their blows are deathly.

At his departure many of us cried, and I joined them. I remembered my children and how much I missed them. Only Sadoun, a peasant and I were left in the cell. Of the people in the passageway only the born-again security agent, who had inherited the doctor's copy of the Qur'an, remained behind. Sadoun took the corner that had been occupied by the trade union member and I sat next to him. But we could no longer talk due to the continuing tyranny of the new guard, who was enjoying his absolute power like a demigod.

The impact of this regime of silence on our nerves was greater than we expected. We would blow up at the slightest provocation, and no one was more affected than Sadoun. This was understandable, as he had spent nine months in that miserable graveyard. I whispered to him that he should try to get some sleep. We were all trying to do that. We felt boredom with every inch of our bodies. Time passed like a tortoise insouciantly sauntering in the desert. Nobody even cared to wipe the ceiling. We missed the beautiful recitations of the doctor at dawn. The former security agent, after a couple of days of preparations and hesitations, tried to claim the doctor's mantle. He had a good voice and fine diction but he was struck with stagefright and did not repeat his performance.

There were many newcomers, but we could no longer ask where they were from or why they had been brought in as the arbitrary authority of the hateful guard forbade speaking. We had been reduced to guessing life stories by looking at the faces of the new prisoners and their bruises, injuries and bloodstained bandages. Their eyes were blurry and sad. The only thing that would be heard from time to time was the defiant recitation of two Qur'anic verses: *There is no authority and power above that of God* and *There are no gods but the one and only God*. Time had ground to a standstill.

At the end of my third month, I was finally called out. A new guard whose eyes were full of malice barked at me:

– You and your personal effects!

Then he walked away.

Despite the draconian regime of silence, Sadoun had been able to write his home number on a piece of paper. He asked me to call his family and reminded me to pretend to faint should they torture me. I did not have much to collect in the way of personal effects, but fishing my shoes out of a huge wooden box containing dozens of pairs took a long time.

To Dahouk

Finally, I was being taken from Mosul to Dahouk. The prison where I had spent the last three months looked like a small room from a distance. It was built on huge white rocks surrounded by a hue of pale red dirt. The whole mountain was decked out in the green shades of an early spring that was at the peak of its beauty. A sea of white and yellow wildflowers offset blood-red wild poppies. No one could dream such beauty. Not even the iron bars of the truck diminished the pleasure I felt then, as I imagined my children playing among the wildflowers. How Abeer would have loved to collect a bouquet!

Three Kurdish prisoners shared the ride. They wore black turbans, and their layered clothes were resistant to cold. We arrived at Dahouk at two in the afternoon. The sun was warm and pleasant, and a few cotton-like fluffs of clouds added to the beauty of an indigo sky.

The huge prison was warmer than the one in Mosul, but the ceilings were as low. It was full of Kurds who sat on spreads and blankets along the walls. As soon as my three fellow travelers entered the room they were rushed by their fellow Kurds, and a rapid torrent of Kurdish started to flow. I greeted everyone in Arabic. Two inmates immediately came to me from the farthest wall.

– Where is the brother from?[1]

– Basra.

There was great joy in the manner of the pair who accosted and interrogated me. Upon hearing that I was from Basra, however, an excited crowd surrounded me and there was no shortage of Kurdish commentary on my fate. Most of them knew no Arabic whatsoever but a few had mastered enough to get by and translated for the others. After they gave up on divining my charges, one of them asked me through one of the interpreters if I had met a certain Hajj Ahmad who owned a hotel in Mosul. A bomb had gone off in his hotel and killed one of the Ansar guerrillas. Another one of the guerrillas was believed to have escaped. The hotel owner had deceived the authorities about the one who had got away by giving them the specifications of the one who had died. After wasting a couple of months, the agents had caught on and arrested him on charges of aiding the guerrillas. I recalled him. He was brought in at seven o'clock at night, right before the big wave had hit. But they had transferred him soon to another prison and I had not seen him after that. Someone asked me if I knew he would be all right. I laughed:

– Can I say that about myself?

I also told them of the huge number of people who were imprisoned in Mosul for missing license plates and they also found it strange.

Most of the inmates in that Dahouk prison were there on capital charges, and they knew that. But they were tough, illiterate, mountain-dwelling men. Their outlook on life was somewhere between fatalistic and nonchalant. More than half of the Kurds diligently prayed at designated times. It was something of an embarrassment that the only three Arabs did not participate. Fortunately for us a number of Kurdish shepherds

---

1. This is the friendly manner in which Arabs of different national and ethnic origins greet each other.

did not pray either. Otherwise, it would have been easy for them to generalize about Arabs as heathens. Certainly this was their impression of all the Arab government officials they had met.[1] Their main charge was aiding the Peshmerga and Ansar guerrillas. In recent months the three main guerrilla groups had inflicted heavy losses on the government forces, which was unprecedented since Barzani's[2] defeat.

One of the Arabs had been a communist who had planned to go underground after their Baghdad headquarters had been raided. But he had been picked up the next morning. He related how the party headquarters in Baghdad had been surrounded. The soldiers cut the electricity and starved them before storming in to kill everyone. This never-reported operation had been carried out in broad daylight and had taken several days.

The other was from Tikrit. I was stunned when I heard this.[3] Upon seeing my amazement, he smiled pleasantly:

– Don't be so surprised. There are many down there who refuse.

He pointed to the south toward Tikrit as he said this.

– They refuse what?

– To become Baath members. But their numbers are diminishing.

– How so?

He craned his neck.

– First, they use bribing. Those who sign up get whatever they wish. A downpour of gold showers them. In my neighborhood

---

1. The Iraqi Baath Party was secular, and before the first Gulf War Saddam Hussein did not profess any religious pretensions.
2. Mullah Mustafa Barzani was the leader of the Kurdish uprising; he was aided by Iran. A rapprochement between Iran and Iraq in 1975 put an end to this support.
3. This town is the birthplace of Saddam Hussein, and due to the tribal nature of his rule almost everyone from this region worked as a high functionary in the government.

alone seven people were given posts in foreign embassies. The most educated among them had graduated from grammar school. The ones who refused ended up like me.

His friend cut in:

– Within six months he was transferred twenty-two times.

I laughed:

– At least you had a job. Not bad.

– In fact, it was not that bad. But do you know how far I traveled in those transfers? I have gone from Safvan in the south to Sulaymaniyah in the north. I traveled eight hundred miles in those six months. As soon as I got to one place there was a telegram waiting for me with orders to report anywhere from Basra to Eij on the Syrian border. When they saw that I did not care, they started locking me up. Usually they did not beat me but made me stand on one foot for half an hour or stare at a blank wall for hours. At first they used to detain me for a few days at a time, but my father would post bail and get me out. The detention kept increasing until I got my first one-month sentence, and then this.

– Did they not tempt you with bribes?

– Oh sure. All I had to do was nod and put my inked finger on the dotted line and I would be a commercial attaché in any embassy I picked.

– A commercial attaché?

– And why not? I am a high-school graduate, while their Leader obtained a grammar school degree through bribes and connections.

– Why *didn't* you put sign on the dotted line?

– Because I believe in the liberty of human beings. Since man has walked the earth he has been free to say and do whatever he wishes. Besides, I do not believe in a system that benefits a few to the point of saturation at the expense of millions who are barely surviving. I shall never stop fighting against such rank injustice. Also, I just know too much about the history of this gang of hooligans to join them.

Among the Kurds there was a senile, elderly man. He could not stand without leaning on something. His prominent hooknose was all the more noticeable amidst the waves of his glistening white beard. How could anyone suspect he could pose a danger to anything or anyone? I mentioned this to the Tikriti.

– Right. Only a coward could have thought that. But he is here in lieu of his *older* brother, who is a suspect!

I was astonished.

– You mean he has a brother even older than he is?

– This one is senile, although he recites the Qur'an from memory without any mistakes. His brother is older by a few years but he is in much better shape, both physically and mentally.

– What is his charge?

– Aiding Amr Abbas.

– Who is Amr Abbas?

– I can't believe you have not heard of him! He was a leftist who went underground before the Baath abrogated its treaties with the leftist parties. He must be in his forties now. He is the leader of the Ansar al-Islam guerrillas in this region. He has been a menace to the regime, though the simple peasant folk tend to embellish his feats.

At the end of June new prisoners were brought in. They were not accused of aiding the guerrillas. Rather, they were the so-called 'nationality Iraqis' or 'Iranian immigrants'. Of course, they were a hundred percent Iraqi. During the Ottoman Empire their ancestors had registered themselves as Iranian immigrants to save their sons from military duty. After national independence they were given Iraqi citizenship and all was forgotten. They lived like the Iraqis that they were until the difficulties between Iran and Iraq started to brew. Then tens of thousands were summarily deported from their homes with hardly the shirts on their backs. Whatever they had inherited and gathered during a lifetime was lost in the blink of an eye.

We did not know why they had been sent to Dahouk from Baghdad and other southern cities where they lived. Later we learned that the highways to the borders in the south were saturated with them and besides, there were military confrontations in the south and middle parts of the border zone. If their treatment during the previous mass deportation was anything to go by, they would be taken to an area some twenty miles from the border and released. Loudspeakers would then blare: 'Go live with your kind.' Walking during the day was possible, despite the frequent rains, but the cold at night would kill many of the elderly and the children. Those who made it would be exhausted and penniless. Whoever tried to return would be immediately arrested. Some would slip back to try and live surreptitiously in the cities. But if they were ever caught, they would be shot on the spot as spies.

A friend of mine in Basra who had seen their trail of tears in the south once described it as 'the Babylonian exile of our times'. He told me they were the most desperate group of people one could ever imagine. Children wilted under the heat of the sun; families could not keep together. It was not uncommon for parents to buy glasses of water for their children for a *dinar* each from police stations. My friend also said he knew of a deportee whose two sisters had committed suicide in Iran by jumping off a four-story building. Their father had been a wealthy man in Kazimain[1] but they had been reduced to eating at soup kitchens and sleeping at mosques in a strange land.

With the coming of the summer the number of prisoners increased, which caused the guards to warehouse some of the inmates in the passageway and near the toilet. The heat was

---

1. A predominantly Shi'ite town in central Iraq.

unbearable, and more impossible to fight than the cold of winter. Waking up every morning I had a sense of self-disgust because my clothes were wet and reeked of sweat. But those who were given a place near the toilet were even worse off due to the ever-present foul smell. We would fantasize about a glass of cold water (relatively cold water was available only in the morning), or for a breath of fresh air or a waft of breeze that was never available. I found it incredible that we had adapted to all this.

With every Baath mercenary dispatched by Ansar al-Islam, the fate of dozens of simple peasant folk danced on the edge of the executioner's blade. Everyone in the direction from which a bullet had come was a suspect: the tailor, the blacksmith, the homeowner. If the identity of a member of the Ansar was discovered, his entire family – including his father, mother and children – was fair game. They once brought in a carpenter because he had not been able to identify a resistance member. He kept asking the same question:

– How I could identify someone I had not seen?

The day the Iraq-Iran war started, we ate our meager breakfast and through the chink in the door spied a lot of guards running around. Some of the inmates were happy, others sad. What we all shared was hunger: they had forgotten to feed us. At seven in the evening we finally got our lunch, which was cold and more inedible than usual. We had heard the word 'war' several times. In case we were in doubt, during the serving of the food a guard ran to us and announced:

– War! War!

On the second day, the officer in charge of political ideology came to pay us a visit. He was short, dark and heavy. His bilious face indicated a difficult childhood. But he tried to pretend to come from privilege. He certainly did his best to look prepared delivering a speech he had obviously rehearsed for hours:

– Some of you are university *griduates* ... I, too, am a *griduate* ...

He horribly mangled the key words, but continued:

– I have successfully finished a forty-two-days program at the university ...

After a long pause, he started to explain the dimensions of the battle against 'the racist, fire-worshipping, Persian enemy' and said that the operations had been thoroughly planned and carefully executed.

– The defeat of the dastardly enemy is a foregone conclusion. It will take twenty or twenty-five days to finish them off. Then a new government will be established in the liberated territories named Arabestan. The provisional officials down to the mayors and village supervisors have already been picked. Should the new liberated Arabestan wish to remain independent, well, why not? They are no less than the Kuwaitis! But if they wish to join the Arab motherland, we will welcome them with open arms. The war is going very well indeed. The Iranians are being tricked, trapped, defeated and pushed around on all fronts.

At this point he decided to extemporize.

– Let me give you an analogy for this war. Who among you has heard the fable of the wolf and the sheep? You know how the wolf was drinking from upstream and tried to pick a fight with a sheep that was drinking from lower down? He told the sheep to stop muddying the water for him, although the sheep could not have done this, as he was downstream. Well, it was just an excuse to pick a fight and devour the sheep.

A few of us who had read the story in the primary school remembered it and noted how inappropriate it was to cast one's own government as the bully wolf. But we remained impassive. No one answered his question. He became nervous, and dug himself in deeper.

– Maybe you will ask me about the position of the United States on this. The Americans have already given us the green light to attack.

Someone whispered:

– A strange admission!

– Since the American Operation Desert One failed, we decided to show the world that we could succeed where they could not. Besides, this will be good training for our final assault on Israel!

Suddenly he appeared at a loss for words, and started to mumble and stutter. Maybe he thought he had said too much, or realized the futility of trying to persuade us. He just stood there, turning shades of purple. He was unable to extricate himself from the situation. Finally he ended his performance with a theatrical military salute, followed by crisp about-face, and marched out. We knew there were spies among us, but this was too good to pass up. Everyone broke out laughing and imitating this ideological burlesque. The Kurds joined the laughter after someone translated what he had said. Then we all started to ponder the dire consequences of a real war for the ordinary people who were already worn out from their daily hardships.

In the following days we received a number of soldiers who had failed to report or deserted. There were also a few who were accused of insubordination or conscientious objection. We tried to ask questions about the conduct of the war but got few answers. Soldiers were usually illiterate and simple-minded, due to the unending draft that had swallowed generations of them. Of the soldiers who had reported late none had received less than five years, but this was not necessarily a bad thing. A military doctor had deliberately refused to report so he could spend his time in jail, rather than at the front. His father had used his connections to reduce his sentence from six to three years, and this made him very happy. He said:

– It is better to be like a buried rock – deaf, dumb and hidden away – than to become a rabid dog and attack others. If you don't take one of these two roads, *poof*! They will wring your neck like a sparrow!

He twisted his hand on his neck for emphasis.

Someone asked me if I would join Ansar al-Islam upon my release. I said I could not think about anything before making sure my children were all right. I longed for them, dreamed about them every night. Who was helping them with their homework? Who was guiding my son, now on the verge of adolescence? What would he say if they asked him about his father at school? Who would help them if they got sick? Tears streamed down my cheeks.

That same night I was called to gather my personal belongings. I wiped my tears and started to say goodbye to everyone. One joker quipped:

– If we had known you were going to leave us, we would have thrown a gala goodbye party and invited Umm Kulthum[1] to perform!

We all laughed. A flood of goodwill poured in from the eyes of the simple Kurdish peasants and the soldiers. I knew I would not see any of them again, which made parting more difficult.

---

1. The renowned Egyptian singer.

To Irbil at a Snail's Pace

I left the Dahouk prison during the afternoon, in a slow-moving truck. The sun was shining on fields of recently-reaped wheat that appeared like the neglected stubble of a derelict. My guard's accent was that of the people of Howayjah.

– Are you from Howayjah?

He answered with impatience and arrogance:

– Yes.

– Are we going back to Mosul?

The reply came back furiously:

– Are you blind? This is not the road to Mosul, but to Irbil!

I had not known there was a road connecting Dahouk and Irbil. They had probably paved it recently for military purposes. The guard appeared nervous and looked around furtively. There were nine of us. Later I learned that one of the prisoners was accused of killing three soldiers. He appeared paralyzed, and was the only one sitting on the floor of the truck, while the rest of us sat on the wooden benches. All the inmates treated the handicapped prisoner with deference. It looked as though he had been tortured to within an inch of his life, but he was silently charismatic; his eyes were strangely bright.

The road to Irbil was long and tortuous. It would be easy to set ambushes, and we had only one guard. I had a creeping suspicion that something was afoot. Such a dangerous prisoner who had killed three soldiers could not have been sent along with only one guard. And why was the truck moving so slowly? As we climbed one of the hills I saw a military convoy following us in the distance. Maybe we were bait to lure Ansar al-Islam guerrillas. What confirmed my theory was that only the door to the prisoners' cage was locked, the other door at the back of the truck left open. I theorized that at the first sign of the Ansar the driver and the guard would jump off and run away. When the guerrillas approached the truck to rescue their comrade, the convoy following us would blow us all up.

Most of the prisoners went to sleep except for an old, dark-skinned man who appeared to never tire of rolling cigarettes with trembling fingers. He was the kind of addict who smokes without the slightest trace of pleasure.

How pleasant was sleep, and even more pleasant, death without pain. Sudden death would be the end of all our suffering, but I thought only of my wife and children. How clever nature is, binding us to an organic fate with filial emotions! How sweet is a cheap death, anytime and anywhere. If the guerrillas came, they might shoot me as a government spy, even if we were not killed instantly by Baath artillery. Whose bullet was better suited to mark a full stop at the end of my life?

In Irbil, we stopped by the garrison. Dozens of civilian cars surrounded us. They looked at us the way one looks at monkeys at the zoo. But some looked with sympathy. It was a few minutes past five in the evening. We were taken to a large yard. Soldiers ran out and emptied the area. Then a few officers gathered about a hundred and fifty feet from us and began an animated debate. One of them motioned to us; the truck started to move out of the yard and parked on the right shoulder of the highway. We were like an exhibit visible to anyone who entered Irbil from Mosul and Dahouk. A soldier who covered his head with a red *yashmak* and hugged a machine-gun climbed in and backed us up, exposing us to the direction of Kirkuk. The guard changed. The new sentry was a fat fellow who did not carry a weapon. As soon as he sat down a flood of obscenities issued from him, describing a bill of deeds of our mothers and ancestors.

The new guard kept leaving his post, as though it was not his duty to keep watch. Hunger was killing us but fear of recriminations kept us all silent. At seven in the evening the weather improved and the heat subsided. We might actually have enjoyed the weather had we had not been extremely hungry. The moonlight adumbrated the distant hills. The truck was parked near a gutter that let the water out of the garrison, an ideal locale for the world's most efficient factory of mosquitoes. The tiny insects attacked us in waves, becoming ferocious beasts and entering our clothes, like fleas, through the smallest of openings. This insult was added to the injury of our starvation. Now I understood why the guard had left his post. The only way out was to wrap oneself in a blanket, but in my case the threadbare wool spread had to do. It was better to sweat a river than be devoured alive.

In the morning the color of the earth had turned very dark, highlighting the bright yellow of the hyacinths. Our faces and hands were puffed out and reddened by the stings of the mosquitoes. I had never realized they could do such damage to human flesh. A middle-aged Kurdish man gathered his courage and spoke in Kurdish to the master sergeant about his hunger, miming and rubbing his hand on his belly. Strangely, the master sergeant did not curse him out. Rather, he quickly brought us a few crusts of bread, filled with uncooked dough, that the soldiers threw away. But we ate every bit, and even enjoyed the bizarre taste of the uncooked dough.

The next day, as we drove toward Kirkuk, the military convoy still followed us at a distance. In Kirkuk the treatment of previous days was repeated, but this time they parked us on the way to Sulaymaniyah and simply forgot about feeding us the entire day. The courageous Kurd asked for food again but the reply was that there was no food anywhere near. There was one restaurant, but it was too far. The pain of starvation forced me to beg the soldier:

— Is it possible that, if we give you some money, you might get us some food tomorrow morning?

The guard, a hard, thin man with red eyes, reacted as though I had insulted him.

— Give us the money afterwards, if you stay here that long.

Instead of laying sandbags, they had raised both sides of the road by six feet. A nine-foot strip of tall dry weed ran along the shoulders of the road. There were no mosquitoes there. The stalks and leaves of the weed were glistening with the drops of rain that had fallen during the previous days. With the coming of the day a group of soldiers crowded around the truck and started to put it on jacks and remove the tires. There was nothing wrong with the truck; this charade was obviously for the benefit of potential Ansar spies.

I winked at the brave Kurd to repeat his request for food and he did. He succeeded again. They brought us some army rations at noon. We asked to be allowed to relieve ourselves, and the red-eyed soldier went to ask for instructions. After half an hour we were let out, one at a time, with an armed escort.

How delicious was the aroma of the earth, saturated with rain. I wanted to jump in the open air and run, to lie down on the ground and kiss it. But the machine gun behind me was quite sobering. We remained in that spot for three days, observed by hundreds and interrogated by dozens of ordinary people. We were dying of starvation. It was clear we were cheap bait by Ansar standards. Maybe we were not any kind of bait at all. We were more like a piece of meat that a dim-witted trapper might use to catch rabbits. The man who was supposed to have killed three soldiers was probably innocent of the charge. Why would Ansar al-Islam risk lives for him?

On the third night, an unseasonable cold wind blew from the northwest and several thunderstorms passed over us. The soldiers' shack was drenched, and so were their supplies. That was a hard and depressing night. Having sat on wooden benches for so long, I felt like I was turning into wood myself.

We had left Dahouk five days earlier and were still in limbo. It was clear that they had not made any plans to feed us; what we did receive was donated by the soldiers from their own rations.

The time passed very slowly. The combination of cold, hunger, darkness and boredom was maddening. My resistance had begun to crumble. I could not stand it anymore. Short arrows of light were dancing in front of me regardless of whether I kept my eyes open or not. Occasional snoozing brought some relief but cold kept waking me up.

I found out that when the body reaches its limit of exhaustion, a wave of peace washes over it. I was finally awash in this peaceful wave, which took me to my wife and children. We were sitting together and laughing. Then I was woken up by the loud sound of something falling on the floor of the truck. The sun was shining, and I was tempted to peek out from my spread; but I kept my eyes shut, hoping to retain a trace of my sweet dream. The loud voices only increased.

– *Rasta Brow!*[1]

A cacophony of cries, sighs and screams followed. The brave old Kurd was crumpled on the floor of the truck with his head between his knees. His usual manner of sitting had not changed. But now he was stiff and cold as an ancient mummy. His turban had rolled off, revealing his thin, greying hair. His unruly stubble

---

1. In Kurdish: 'As you like, brother.'

appeared messier than before. But his eyes remained prominent. They were limpid, calm and teasingly ironic. Although his face had a natural tan, his legs appeared yellowish, almost gilded. The soles of his feet and his toes were dirty and deeply cracked.

We forgot all of our other miseries and gathered around him. A sluggish guard rubbed his eyes and looked at the corpse with indifference. Then a second and a third arrived, and soon there were more than ten of them. They started to argue in loud Kurdish and Arabic.

– So, what is the big deal? Dozens die at the front every day.

– Cover him up with a blanket.

– There are no blankets.

– What did he use as a cover?

– Nothing.

– Wait.

After a few minutes one of them came back with a blanket with huge food stains and patches of dried-up dirt. He threw the blanket into the truck. The blanket would have landed on the corpse had someone not caught it in midair. One of the Kurds, who was of the same age as the dead man, made an oblique protest to this irreverence toward the dead

– *There is no power above that of God.*

The ruggedness of a tough life had left the dead body. It appeared shrunken as though dressed up in the clothes of a man much bigger than him. The other elderly Kurd shook and rubbed the dirty blanket with a frowning face. Others helped place the body on its side and put the turban under his head.

– *In the name of God, the beneficent, the merciful. Thou, righteous, peaceful soul. Come back to thy Lord well pleased and well pleasing unto Him. Enter thou, among My devotees, enter thou My heaven.*[1]

---

1. These verses conclude Chapter 89 (*al-Fajr*) of the Qur'an, and are often recited at funerals.

The old Kurd finished the recitation, closed the corpse's eyes and covered his face. A man in his thirties with an overhanging moustache sobbed. The rest of us were brooding.

In Solomon's Dungeons

We finally reached Sulaymaniyah and entered a newly constructed building from the rear, situated in a narrow street. Dark, ominous faces and hellish eyes greeted us. I started to tremble with anxiety and tried to look away from the barrels of the machine guns. With every loud noise we jumped and prepared for the worst. Finally a youthful security agent climbed onto the back of the truck and locked the gate behind him. After another fifteen minutes the truck moved toward a huge walled compound. Two gates that could have accommodated two trucks at once opened for us. About ten prisoners were added to our company, and we set out again.

I felt I could not endure hunger any more. It was thirty hours since I had had a crust of bread. Several times I decided to ask the guard for food, but my pride prevented me from doing so. When the truck started to move my hunger increased even more. Around two-thirty in the afternoon I gave up hope that we would stop for the guards' lunch break. I could no longer follow the conversation of my fellow inmates. I could hear words and understand them but was unable to connect them together, but did not care anymore. I was losing my mind. I felt as though I had fallen; it hurt just a bit, but I felt a sense of bliss. Happiness rained on me from every direction. Life had little to offer to lure me back.

I don't know how long I remained unconscious. I started to hear words again: 'food', 'hungry' … 'thirsty' … 'exhausted'. I opened my eyes, and a clear, smiling face with thin lips said:

– You are running a fever. Eat.

I saw a red bowl in which was placed a steaming peace of meat and an onion.

– Eat. You will feel better.

I ate to satiety. At first glance, I had thought that the food in the bowl would not be enough, but I was unable to finish it. Then I drank a cup of tea and closed my eyes. They had put a carpet on the floor of the truck and given me a pillow. I slept only to be plunged into horrific nightmares. I saw the face of our dead companion. I thought he was under the blanket with me, pulling the blanket with his toes from over my legs. When I touched his body I found it was as cold as ice, shivered and woke up. The truck had stopped.

– He is sick with fever. He cannot get up.

But I did get up, fearing that if I tarried I would be harassed. I leaned on one of the prisoners and got off the truck. The night had dropped its black curtains, and the pale stars would be sending their light through in a little while. The breeze was pleasant. It was a little after six. Names were read, but mine was not among them. Then a man in civilian clothes pointed at me and said:

– Is he the one?

A shiver trickled down my spine. The prisoners were gone and I was standing alone in a yard, staggering and about to collapse. The truck that had brought me was gone. I fumbled for something to lean on. What was the meaning of this? Where was I, and why was I brought here? Let them do what they want, I thought. To hell with them. I could not hold my balance, and squatted.

– Get up.

– He is sick. He will die.

– Get up.

Someone was kicked. Was it I who was being kicked? It appeared so, but it did not hurt at all. I had the strange feeling he was just roughhousing with me. But I was sent rolling as a result. I got to my feet and staggered again. Finally my time had come, after ten months. The will to stand was really just a matter of prudence. My eyelids were shutting. I fell into a deep sleep.

– What is your name?

I opened my eyes. A short, white youth with well-groomed hair in the style of the ancient Romans was interrogating me. Where did they find these handsome henchmen? In the time of the King these types had faces so ugly, even a mother could not love them. But they were less cruel. Next to him stood another good-looking man with a very thick but slightly greying beard. Nobody had asked my name for a long time. I had almost forgotten it.

– Mustafa Ali Noman.

– What is the nature of your relationship with the Peshmerga guerrillas?

My body and clothes were wet with perspiration. The room was empty of furniture. I sat on a bamboo chair. Three feet behind me was a wall from which strange electrical cables were hanging. A foul, chemical smell hung in the air. I guessed that it was what they had used to wake me up. My head was still heavy. Four lengths of thick rope attached to blocks of wood were hanging from the ceiling and the opposite wall featured metal plates covered with electric wires and colored lights. I remembered the advice of my fellow inmates that I should exaggerate my pain and pretend to pass out. But how could I pretend to anything? I did not have the energy to form a coherent sentence, much less scream. My mouth was full of foam, but I had no idea where it came from. My tongue felt heavy and immobile as though sewn to the roof of my mouth. They were starting to think I was unable to speak but I finally managed to answer the question.

– What relationship can a simple employee have to the Peshmerga?

– We ask the questions around here! What is the nature of your relationship with them?

My throat dried up and my voice turned to a whisper. I mimed that I needed some water.

– Bring him some damn water.

I took a sip and continued.

– I have no relationship with the Peshmerga. Bring a witness, and if he testifies against me, then kill me.

My throat dried up again, and I thought that I was failing to communicate what was in my mind. Where were the thousands of imaginary defenses that I had prepared during the gloomy, sleepless nights? They had all evaporated. The question was repeated and I responded in the same manner. Then they pulled out a photograph about one-quarter the size of a postcard.

– Isn't this your face? Can you deny that?

– Yes, it is me.

– And who is this guy standing behind you?

The man they were referring to was tall and appeared older than me by a few years. He wore a plaid shirt and a reassuring smile. I was sitting at a long table playing cards. On my right there was a man dressed in the outfit of mountain Kurds, and on my left stood a short middle-aged man with close-cropped hair and a square moustache. He appeared to be talking to me. Where was this? The memories came in a rush.

– Answer.

It was taken in Sarsang, after the defeat of the Barzani uprising, years ago. Yes … I used to visit the casino at around nine o'clock at night and proceed to the al-Wassin wing, to a long poker table that seated fifteen people. On my second visit I greeted the middle-aged man who had sat next to me the previous day, and he invited me to a cup of tea. I told him he had made a couple of mistakes in the game the day before. He thanked me and insisted that I join him in a game some time. That was it. But I had never seen the man standing behind me. He must have been under constant surveillance. But who was he? I soon found out he was their most-wanted man, their number-one bogeyman, the notorious Amr Abbas.

– Why is he standing behind you? And besides, why did you go on vacation this year exactly on the month of October?

– October … Why? Well, because I had to complete my house. I had had enough of renting. I took time off to finish my house.

– Interesting. And at the same time Amr Abbas happened to be in Basra and stole a container of munitions from a ship anchored in the Shatt al-Arab. There is no use in denying it. It is best if you confess. At the very least you will not be tortured. Sheer coincidence cannot account for all this evidence.

So a reckless night of fun from youth had come back to hound me to the gates of hell. The small candle of hope that had glimmered during my captivity extinguished. Now, I told myself. Try to think of freedom if you dare. Try to remember the faces of your children one last time. Remember your wife. The innocent laughter in the house, the joy in their eyes, their smiles. Let these burn in your mind as your last impression of this life as they tighten the noose around your neck. Remember your wedding, now, as your death comes 'closer than two throws of a stone'.[1]

---

1. This quote alludes to the *al-Najm* chapter of the Qur'an (Chapter 53, Verse 9).

The interrogation was long and nerve-wracking. The repetition of questions, and my exhaustion, made me easy prey for their traps. A child would have laughed at the statements I made. But what did it matter? To hell with it all. Let them do what they want, I thought. I felt I was growing stupider. I felt numb. My two interrogators grew in dimension. I saw them as a couple of giants seen in a concave mirror. I must have fallen on my right side. I was burning inside, though I felt like I was swimming in the sea. But I was afloat in a muddy cesspool. I saw blinking lights.

– We will start tomorrow. This is the fifth time he has passed out.

In fact, I was conscious when they carried me back to my cell, dragging me by my hands and feet. The passageway was dark. The person holding my legs must have felt tired, and let go.

– Let's just drag him by his hands.

– But he might die ...

– To hell with him.

I opened my eyes in a cold, dark cell furnished with a single blanket. Mine was one of four cells in a room illuminated by the weak, yellow light of a single bulb. Before being divided to accommodate four prisoners, it must have been an ordinary room; each cell could fit only one person. Iron bars divided the room into a quad of cells with enough space in front of the door for a guard to sit holding his weapon. A waist-high sheet of metal covered the iron bars around each cell. If the inmates had been allowed to stand, they would have seen each other. But of course, standing was forbidden. We were made to wear a black, foul-smelling and suffocating hood when we had to go to the toilet.

I do not recall how long I spent in this prison as I ran a high fever during my stay there. The fever would give way to sweating, and I would shake with such terrible intensity that the metal walls separating the cells would also rattle. This caused the irritable guard – whose health had obviously suffered from the rigors and unusual hours of a career in torture – to curse me out:

– If you must shake, stay away from the walls! You're making a racket!

I just repeated the Qur'anic verse:

– *There is no power except that of God.*

– Shut up, you and your lot of your jackasses, your Khomeini and Da'wa and Prophet Muhammad and God!

Due to the small size of my cell, I could not help causing walls to vibrate when I was afflicted with the shakes. Yet, my illness was a blessing, as it saved me in my first interrogation by causing me to pass out repeatedly. It was also helpful in my second interrogation.

They put the black sack on my head and took me away with my hands tied behind my back. The demand to confess was followed by a blow to the face that rattled my jaws. The blow was so hard I could not fully close my mouth and bring my teeth together for two months afterwards. I felt the blood flowing from my nostrils. It alternately felt hot and cold. I did not know why. Perhaps my illness increased my pain threshold. As my blood soaked the hood I understood where the foul smell came from. Again I forgot to feign passing out. I could also have used one of those shaking fits; but I had no such luck, but I must have blacked out for a while, because I found myself standing without knowing how I got there. Another blow caused me to stagger backward, but instead of falling back a strong kick sent me forward. I fell on my face.

– Get up.

I found it hard to stand with my hands tied behind my back. I felt the heat of my fever. I was bleeding and crying at once. The kicks continued to rain on me where I was lying.

– Get up.

As soon as I was up, another kick brought me down on my face.

– Get up.

My mouth was dry, and although I was wailing with pain, the sack on my head muffled my voice.

– Get up.

I tried to stand, but failed. One of the torturers helped me up this time. He then attached my handcuffs to something and I felt a pull. Soon I was suspended from the ceiling. I screamed in the hood with all of my might. I had the sensation that my shoulder was about to be separated from my body. Luckily, they let me down after a minute or so.

– Why are you still dressed? Take off his clothes.

I must have made a sight to behold. Not even a cartoon character could be dressed so ridiculously. I had a black sack on my head and wore a shirt and a tie, but was naked from the waist down. They amused themselves burning my pubic hair for a while. The burnt smell filled the room. Finally, when they started beating me with a water hose, I threw up and passed out.

I was woken up with another kick and prepared for another pleasure ride with the sack and the handcuffs and the rest. But I was thrown a crust of bread and two small, cold kebabs to eat. I realized I was in my cell, and that it was evening, because kebabs were served. The kind of food served was our only means of gauging time.

The only thing worse than torture is the pain that follows it. I was sore all over, but my infected and raw burns were the worst. I could sleep only on one side. My burns had turned really messy. Feverish sleep was my only relief. When I was awake I wailed and wept, unable to control myself. It was clear my neighbors suffered similar pain. The wailing never stopped. Occasionally two prisoners would harmonize their wailing, as though one was answering the other, creating weird musical phrases. I don't believe the cries ever stopped. I did not understand how the guard could take it all.

I have no idea how many days I spent in this jail, as I was in a constant hellish trance from sickness compounded by torture. My hands were almost paralyzed; as soon as I tried to use them, unbearable pain would sting my shoulders. My hands had become strangers to me.

Probably after ten days I was decked out in the black sack again. Anxiety got the better of me. I could not move my feet. My hands were in cuffs, behind my back. I remembered my family, and tears flowed anew. Petrified and trembling, I was sure I was walking to my death. The wounds would hurt terribly if opened. The guard pushed me forward violently. Finally he took my forearm, and we stopped. I heard another voice:

– Enter … Take off the sack.

My heart was beating hard, and I was a panting, nervous wreck. A man in his thirties with light hazel eyes and a double chin, his brown hair streaked with gold, pointed to my guard. I did not dare to look in that direction. He took off my handcuffs; I automatically heaved a sigh of relief. Then I was led by the hand to sit in front of the officer. The room was elegant, but I was astonished to see a bunch of fresh flowers in a vase. How could someone like him enjoy flowers? I saw his name plaque: Major Muhammad Salah. His bookcases were full of titles obviously confiscated from raids on leftists' homes. The room also sported a picture of the Leader, as well as his instructions to the security forces in shiny gold frames.

– Don't you know that we need your help?

I did not know how to respond. Power, authority, law, right and wrong were all on his side. What did I have to appeal to? He continued:

– Why don't you help yourself?

I trembled.

– How?

He smiled. Now he was hovering over me.

– Confess.

My germinating hopes were nipped. But I found courage, too. I screamed with all my might:

– You said you would help me! Either tell me how I can prove my innocence, or keep me here until you find the person you are looking for! If he testifies against me as an accomplice, then kill me! Just because a man stood behind me fifteen years ago, I stand accused today?! Just because my time off coincides with the theft of explosives, I am responsible?! I can bring you a thousand alibis that I never left the site of my building for the duration of that time! By keeping me here you are failing to arrest the real culprit!

He laughed, and trailed off into a smile.

– We are convinced that you have not done anything wrong. There has been a mistake regarding your name, but you must prove that you have nothing to do with your poker partner.

His statement caused an ebb and flow in my hopes for release. First they had focused on Amr Abbas, but now there was a question of my poker partner.

– How can I prove that? Why don't you look him up in the records?

– We want to hear it from your lips.

I shook my head.

– I cannot remember the name of a man I saw five minutes ago. But I remember faces ...

– Very well. Where is your home in Basra?

I answered him. He asked me about a man who sold wine in my neighborhood. This man had 'very liberated' daughters, and his house was frequented by high officials of the regime. The youngest woman was a student at the university; I had been amazed that she could combine an intellectual life with another one so sordid. Finally, I had been forced to decouple intellectual poverty and unsavory activities.

He was indulging in distant reveries.

– Basra! That is one beautiful city … Are you a member of the Baath?

– Yes. I am a supporter.

– You joined during a recent membership campaign, didn't you?

– Yes.

– Then without the campaign you would not be a member, right?

– …

– Don't tell anyone what happened here.

– Oh! Never!

– You are lucky I like the people of Basra.

His eyes grew dreamy again. Then he pointed at me to leave. I rose in disbelief, and was about to fall, but the guard caught me. He put the sack on my head again but did not handcuff me. Why the sack if I was so close to being released?

I could not fight the cold of February with a single blanket and my threadbare spread. But the hope of freedom had revived me. I started to use my hands as life slowly returned to them. My wounds started to heal, too. After a week I filled out release forms. Then I was ordered to shave, sit in front of a huge camera and have my picture taken. Ten days later I was taken to the Major again, and he smiled as though he had done me a great favor.

– We will send your papers to the head investigator. They will come back in a few days. Where do you want to be released, in Baghdad or in Basra?

– Release me from *here*!

I blurted that out impetuously, in a loud voice. I remembered the rigors of traveling in army trucks all too well.

– Then you must heal completely before you can be released.

The Last Sojourn

I was taken out from a new exit this time, with no sack on my head. I entered a jail that resembled the usual security facilities everywhere, except it was bigger. It was well-lit with natural light and had clean toilets.

A youth with smooth, dark skin and very dark eyes greeted me. His hair was neatly combed. Judging from his long hair, good manners and looks, I guessed he was an important merchant. But I found out he was actually a baker from Karbala. Six months earlier he had returned from Kuwait, but was arrested at the airport because his name was identical to that of the economics minister, who had escaped. When he told security officers he was illiterate and had no diplomas of any kind, they took that as an insult to their intelligence and locked him up.

He had been in the same quad room with me. As he was tall, he had been able to see into other cells even from a sitting position. He said I was moaning all the time, and so loudly that I drowned out the call to prayer in the morning. This had caused the guards to report my situation to the higher-ups. I was surprised, as I believed I had controlled myself and not bothered others too much. He told me that the other two who were with us had died under torture, and that we were to thank God we got away with our lives. There were about thirty people in the security jail. Most of them were policemen and soldiers calmly waiting to be tried for crimes that would usually bring life sentences. Two were members of the People's Militia and a few were important party members. There were four merchants and three others who were awaiting trial for inciting prisoners to go on a hunger strike.

Two of the merchants were accused of aiding the Iranian revolution, but they said they had owed money to the deported 'Iranian immigrants'. (As religious men they had felt compelled to pay personal debts, especially when their former creditors were in dire need.) The third had sent his children to Switzerland to avoid the draft. Finally, one merchant was to be tried for refusing to join the exiles into Iran in order to spy on them.

The military inmates were there for more amusing reasons. The youngest of them had fired a missile at a plane, which landed instead on a center belonging to the People's Militia. Many were serving time for shooting off their mouths. A corporal from Basra had got drunk and said: 'Everyday "he" invites another goat from the goats of Africa and fills his pockets with millions while people are killing for a piece of fruit. Many have not been able to afford a single banana in years.' Another had said: 'It is boorish to smoke a cigar on formal occasions, especially for a man whose father could only afford to smoke cow dung.' A lieutenant had obliquely criticized the Leader for his practice of decorating himself with military honors. Another lieutenant had been thrown in jail for expressing dismay at the Iraqi practice of looting Iranian cities and selling the goods on the streets of Basra. There was also a soldier arrested because he had expressed doubt that the war against Iran would end in one week. The most interesting case was that of a colonel who had bantered with others in the Officers' Club. He had snapped his fingers at a waiter and said: 'Give him a thousand *dirhams*.' This was interpreted as mocking the manners of the Leader. But there were rumors that he had also cursed Haroun al-Rashid.[1] A couple of teenagers conscripted into the People's Army would hang around the military group. One of them, who had had his fill of cold and hunger, had cursed 'whoever got him into this mess' at the Muhammarah front – though he had been careful enough to also curse his own father and brothers to save them from collective punishment. The other had actually shot himself in the foot to avoid fighting. He would often ask questions and answer himself before giving others a chance to venture a guess:

– What do you think is the punishment for what I have done? Huh? Execution, of course! I have asked many, many people!

The soldiers were relatively relaxed. But the policemen were quite uptight. They still acted in rigid military style and observed the hierarchy among themselves. But when they were alone, one could approach them. I once asked their superior officer about his reason for being there. He had witnessed the killing of thirteen Iranian prisoners of war by a firing squad. After the execution the officer in charge had gone over to a seventeen-year-old soldier and touched the barrel of his weapon:

– This is cold. Why didn't you shoot?

– I cannot shoot a Muslim in captivity.

The officer had put a bullet in the soldier's head on the spot. The police sergeant then objected that the soldier should have been arrested and court-martialed.

I asked how he had dared to object to the summary execution. He said that the officer could not have got away with killing two people. After a pause he added:

– Besides, I would have killed him first if he had reached for his weapon.

The Baath Party members were a distinct group. They stayed together and avoided politics as much as they could. But they

---

1. The famous *caliph* of the Abbasid Dynasty (reigned 786–809 AD), with whom Saddam Hussein identified himself.

were big on jokes. Nothing was sacred to them, as though they knew that the business of life and death was just a game. One of them told me he was sure my case was one of mistaken identity, and that the photograph they had shown me had been doctored to cover up their mistake.

I had once asked myself: 'Everybody seems to fear the Baath. But whom does the Baath fear?' I found the answer during my last sojourn in Baath prisons. They feared two things and they feared them more than stray dogs fear rocks flung at them. The first were the so-called 'reports'. They were addicted to writing reports, not only on their colleagues but also on members of their own family, friends and neighbors. They were supposed to be specific in these reports, so they had to produce things like license plate numbers and specific times and places. This mandatory practice was the cause of a pestilence of reports that buried everyone. They feared these reports that they were turning out day and night at the expense of their humanity and honor. A comrade had reported her husband, charging him with disapproving of her late return from Party meetings. Another had betrayed his own friend as being a tad fanatical in practicing religious rites. The said friend had been liquidated during the first week of war. A teacher had reported her own brother on a similar charge and he, too, had been executed. The writers of these reports, however, were rapidly promoted in the Party.

The second thing that frightened the Baath members was the future. A subliminal consciousness of their transitory power seemed to feed their greed for immediate gratification and luxuries. They all had plans for escape in the event of an abrupt end to their reign. In the words of one of the merchants, they followed an alternative interpretation of the famous saying of Imam Ali: *Live for the regime as though it will last eternally, but smuggle your money to foreign accounts as though they it will collapse tomorrow.*[1] One of them once confided to me:

– Death awaits us wherever we go. If the executioner here does not get us, the resistance – be it Kurdish, Shi'ite or leftist – will.

This was evidence that even the members of the Party were not as thoroughly brainwashed as I had thought.

Before the war the majority of prisoners were political. But since the onset of the war, military personnel comprised the majority. Because of the fresh supply of new prisoners, we had access to information about the progress of the war, unavailable to ordinary people. Prisoners were also privileged because they were safe. The small jail was by far safer than the large prison out there. If the government had gone through the trouble of observing me for two months before making sure I was not involved in any political activities, then nobody was safe. Sooner or later everybody was liable to run afoul of the regime or be mistaken for someone who had. This meant that everyone was in line to undergo and suffer all that I had. Being free only meant one thing: imminent arrest. I decided that if I were to be arrested again it would not be for nothing. I decided never to give myself up, like a sheep going to the slaughterhouse.

This resolution ran through my mind as I was released one day to run freely on the other side of the iron bars. When and how and where would I strike back at those who struck me, humiliated me, trampled on my pride, caused my children to suffer and violated my humanity? They could do all this just because they had usurped the power as we were asleep.

After fifteen months away from my family, I could not wait any longer. The joyful prospect of seeing them was sweeping me off my feet and washing over me like tidal waves. But I was not

---

1. The saying is: *Live your life in this world as though you will be here forever, but prepare for the hereafter as though you will die tomorrow.*

sure if my happiness would last. It just happened that the day of my release fell on Monday. *Dad, is it true that on the Prophet's birthday nothing bad happens to children?*

As I ran I clasped my meager personal effects. I just wanted to put distance between that quagmire and myself. I lost track of time. I found myself in an ordinary street with houses, stores, trees, and pavements. I was indeed free. The fangs of a snake dripping with venom had closed on me, but I had managed to escape with my life. Who would believe this? I leaned on a wall, panting. My smile filled the universe. I was free.

How do I know that I am not dreaming this? Pinch myself? No. There is the proof: a young man is walking his motorcycle, on which he is balancing a cannister of gas. He looks exhausted by the chores of ordinary life. The town square is exploding with spring flowers, each singing of hope against an azure sky embroidered with puffs of white, cottony clouds. How utterly beautiful is the sight of municipal workers sitting on the pavement and smoking, under the dancing palm fronds. A garbage can lies overturned. Cars pass by with a monotonous hum. A waft of cold air at once intoxicates me and makes me shiver. Isn't this all enough? I smile, I laugh, I sing, I scream, I dance.

This is the end of all fears.

Must get a grip. I wish I could take pictures of my feelings. I would stop time to record the joy of seeing my wife and family, to take a picture of the rainbow that is blooming in me. I tremble. How will I greet them? How will they greet me? My tears are streaming down my cheeks in anticipation. I am alive and free: a miracle.

I pick up a rock and let my fingers drink its coolness, its hardness. I envelop it in my palm and press my fingers around it. I touch Nature. A seven-year-old boy looks at me. He is carrying a big, plastic basket, somewhat overacting his labors. He sees me and is scared: a man holding a rock and crying. He thinks I am crazy. I smile at him; I want to hug him. I want to hug everything. I drop the rock and keep walking, keep flying on the wings of my imagination. The moment of happiness is within reach. Now the star of happiness has risen in an indigo sky.